DEAD WEIGHT

By
FRANK KANE

I0616803

ARMCHAIR FICTION
PO Box 4369, Medford, Oregon 97504

*For more information about Armchair Books and products, visit our
website at...*

www.armchairfiction.com

Or email us at...

armchairfiction@yahoo.com

"GET IN MY WAY AND I'LL STAMP YOU FLAT!"

That's what the boss of Chinese Heaven told Johnny Liddell. "You'll tell me what I want to know—sooner or later." The gunman swept the flat of the barrel across Johnny's cheek. "You asked for it, peeper… We'll see how tough you are." A switch knife flashed in the goon's hand.

Everyone was threatening Johnny Liddell, even his girl and the cops, until Johnny came up with a new kind of twist to trap a killer. It was so good that he fooled everyone—even himself!

Carried out in the heart of Chinatown, this gritty mystery has it all: Torture, murder, conspiracy… A must read for all Yellow Peril fans and a definite hit—in more ways than one—for any whodunit enthusiast!

POLICE LINEUP:

JOHNNY LIDDELL
A PI who'd gained some fame working in Frisco's Chinatown; he was now on the East Coast—working for a dead guy!

RONNY "MUGGSY" KIELY
A crackerjack reporter with an inside line on murder—she wasn't about to let this story get away from her.

INSPECTOR HERLEHY
Aware of Liddell's PI abilities he was willing to give him some leeway. Then people started dying…a lot of people.

GOLDY LATOUR
This dame was something else. An old hooker, A-number-1 in the art of flimflam, she ran her gig from downtown to uptown.

JIMMY KAIMING
Leader of the East Coast tong, he appeared especially interested in the murder of his countryman—someone he didn't even know.

BEN CERLA
Gambler and racketeer man, he was truly bad news. His presence in Chinatown could only mean more trouble.

HUNT BRIN
He was a swindler of the socialite type—hard to pin a number on him, but not so hard to scare him into talking.

CHAPTER ONE

JOHNNY LIDDELL LEANED BACK in his desk chair, watched the shadow on the corridor side of the frosted-glass door that proclaimed: *Johnny Liddell—Private Investigations—Entrance Room 825.*

It was a man's shadow. A small man's. It stood undecided for a moment, then headed down the corridor in the direction of *Entrance Room 825.*

Liddell sighed, crumpled the paper drinking-cup, tossed it at the wastebasket. It hit the rim, bounced off, rolled on the floor. Liddell stared at it glumly, mentally debated the necessity for keeping the place clean, won the decision, stayed where he was. He replaced the fifth of bourbon in the bottom drawer of the new desk, pulled a pile of old correspondence in front of himself, and was apparently ears-deep in work when the redhead from the front office stamped in.

There was a pink flush of annoyance on her face. "There's a Mr. Liddell to see you, Mr. Liddell. A Mr. Johnny Liddell."

Liddell considered the announcement, shrugged. "Let's have a look at him, Pinky."

"Mr. Liddell will see you now, Mr. Liddell," the redhead snapped over her shoulder. She glared as the little man sidled into the room, flounced past him, and slammed the door after her.

The shadow hadn't lied. Its owner was a small man. Small and old. He seemed lost in the folds of the shapeless overcoat he wore, and only the protrusion of his ears kept his battered fedora from sliding down over his eyes. It was an old face, the skin like transparent parchment, but the eyes were alert, glistening like black beads from behind the folds of his eyelids. He was Chinese.

"You are Johnny Liddell?" The voice was harsh, sibilant, softened only by the smile that accompanied it. "The Johnny Liddell who worked in California nine or ten years ago?"

Liddell nodded. "That's me. Which one are you?"

The old man chuckled. He pulled the fedora off his head, baring a high, hairless dome. "I hope you don't mind my borrowing your name. It was the first one to come to mind." He placed a paper-wrapped package on the corner of the desk, covered it with the fedora. "Not quite so insulting, I think, as John Smith or John Doe, eh?"

Liddell shrugged. "Forget it. I never took out a copyright on the name. What's on your mind?"

The old man pulled a chair close to the desk, dropped wearily into it. "I want you to keep something for me." He indicated the package on the corner of the desk.

Liddell sighed. He found a pack of cigarettes in his top drawer, held it out to the old man, waited until he had selected one, then hung one from the corner of his own mouth, where it waggled when he talked.

"Why not a safe deposit or a checkroom?"

The old man lit his cigarette, held it to his lips between thumb and index finger, squinted at Liddell through the smoke. "It will be safer here than in a public checkroom, and it will be available at any time, not just during banking hours."

"Okay. So you want me to keep a package for you. What else?"

"Nothing else." The old man reached into his pocket, dragged out a worn leather wallet, fumbled through it nearsightedly, came up with two fifties. "This will be sufficient?"

Liddell glanced at the bills, raised his eyebrows. "A hundred just to board a package?" He reached over for the package and weighed it in his hand. "What's the gimmick?"

The old man smoked placidly. "I don't understand."

"Neither do I. Why should you want to pay me a hundred dollars just to drop this thing into my safe for a couple of weeks or even a month?"

"I thought I had explained," the old man told him patiently. "It is worth much to me, much more than this," he waved a hand at the bills on the desk, "to know that this package is safe and that I can pick it up at a moment's notice." He pulled himself out of the chair and stood at the far side of the desk. The cigarette hung precariously in the exact center of his mouth. "There is nothing more?"

Liddell shook his head. "On your way out, the redhead will give you a receipt. Leave your name and address with her in case I have to get in touch with you."

A benign grin wrinkled the parchment of the yellow face. "I do not need a receipt. I trust you." He picked up the battered fedora, jammed it down over the shining pate until it came to rest on his ears. "It is not important for you to know where to find me, as long as I know where to find you." He nodded, turned, and walked to the door with a queer, shuffling motion.

Liddell watched the reception room door close behind the narrow shoulders of his visitor. A few seconds later the thin shadow reappeared on the frosted-glass door briefly, headed in the direction of the elevator bank. Liddell picked up the desk phone, pushed down a button on its base. The redhead's voice came through.

"Call Joe down in the cigar stand in the lobby, Pinky. Give him a good description of the guy who just left here," Liddell told her. "If he takes a cab, I want to know who the cabby was. If he walks, I want him tailed. And if he has a car, I want the license plate number."

"Will do," the receiver chirped back.

Liddell dropped the receiver back on its hook, picked up the package, turned it over in his hands curiously. It was wrapped in a heavy brown paper, its edges sealed with a red wax imprinted with a peculiar seal. It measured about four inches wide by about nine long, and was no more than a quarter of an inch thick. He was still puzzling over it when the door opened and the redhead came in.

"Joe says he'll take care of that, Johnny." She dropped into the chair the little Chinese had used. "Thought he was pretty cute, didn't he? Using your name... What was the idea?"

Liddell scowled. "He was testing me."

"What do you mean, testing you?"

"He wanted to see how good I was. See if I was smart enough to detect he was using an alias," he growled. He opened the top drawer of the desk, tossed the paper-wrapped package in, locked the drawer with a small key on his chain. "I guess I passed the test. He hired me to play nursemaid to a package."

"What kind of package?"

"Just a package." He crushed his cigarette out in the metal ashtray on the corner of the desk. "This sure is a helluva way for a grown man to make a living."

"I don't know what you're kicking about. You've only had your own agency for a month or so and already you've had at least ten jobs. Is that bad?"

"What kind of jobs? Watching tin coffeepots at a wedding. Twice. Two dames who wanted to know where their husbands spent their evenings, three guys ditto their wives. Now I'm playing bodyguard to a paper package. You call that good?" He got up from behind the desk, stamped over to the screen in the corner, pushed it aside, ran some water into the basin. "If I don't get some honest-to-God action soon I'm going to join the Boy Scouts just for excitement." He splashed some water in his face, sputtered.

"Going out again?" the redhead asked incuriously.

Liddell swabbed his face dry with the towel, hung it back on the rack. "You're damn right. If I hang around here any longer, I'll go stir-crazy."

"Where can I get hold of you if I need you?"

Liddell resisted the impulse to annoy the redhead, dragged a comb through his thick hair. "Mike's place on Forty-fourth Street."

Pinky nodded. "I thought so. You're giving that place quite a play these days. What's the attraction?"

Liddell shoved the screen back in front of the basin, adjusted his tie. "It's the only place in town where I can feel like a detective any more. I keep my hand in trying to see how many times I can spot the bartender beating the cash register!"

The bar at Mike's Deadline Café was lined two-deep with refugees from the ad agencies that fill the neighboring skyscrapers. Most of them wore the full-dress uniform of the account executive, the gray striped suit and black knitted tie, and held in their hand the badge of their profession, the dry Martini.

Johnny Liddell leaned on the end of the bar with the ease born of long experience, added to the gray fog that swirled lazily near the ceiling. He examined his glass, found it empty, and signaled for a refill as he watched the bartender stab at the keys of the cash register and dump in a handful of change.

The man behind the stick made a production out of dumping a few ice cubes into a glass, drenching them down with bourbon. He separated a quarter and a half from the pile of change on the bar in front of Liddell, shuffled off to answer a phone that had started shrilling somewhere.

Liddell took a sip of the bourbon; softened it with a touch from the water pitcher.

"It's for you, Liddell," the bartender called down from the other end of the bar.

Liddell grabbed his glass, shouldered his way down to where the bartender stood holding the receiver. He took it, held his hand over the mouthpiece. "I make it three-sixty since I been sitting here, Joe. Not counting my seventy-five cents that hasn't been rung up yet."

The bartender grinned, glanced around, lowered his voice. "Wrong. Should be four-thirty. You musta missed a couple of quarters and the two dimes on the last round. You're slipping, Liddell."

Liddell growled under his breath. "What a detective! Can't even see it when it's being done right in front of my face." He took a sip from the glass, held the receiver to his ear.

It was the redhead in the office. She sounded upset.

"You better get right on back, Johnny. There's trouble."

"What kind of trouble? The poodle I got back for the fat dame got fleas or something?"

The receiver sounded worried. "Real trouble. There are some men here. Federal men. They've got a search warrant."

"A search warrant? What are they after?"

The receiver hesitated. "They've got some sort of idea there was a man here this morning who left a package. They want the package."

Liddell nodded. "I'll be right up, Pinky. Tell them not to go away."

The man sitting in Liddell's chair behind the desk was a stranger. He made no move to get up when Johnny Liddell walked in. He had an unlighted cigar clenched between his teeth, his eyes were cold and unfriendly.

"I hear you boys wanted to see me. Hope I didn't keep you waiting."

The man behind the desk shook his head. He rolled the cigar from one corner of his mouth to the other. "Not too long."

"What's the beef?" Liddell wanted to know. He looked from the man behind the desk to the two hard-eyed men sprawled in chairs near the door.

"They've got a search warrant, Johnny," the redhead told him. "They wanted to break open your top drawer, but I asked them not to smash up the new furniture."

"Mind if I see the warrant?"

The man behind the desk pursed his lips, shrugged. "Not at all." He pulled a legal-looking paper from his pocket, slid it across the desk. From his side jacket pocket he pulled a worn leather case, flipped it open, flashed a metal shield at Liddell. "I'm Byers. Treasury Department."

Liddell nodded, dropped the warrant on the desk. "What's it all about?"

Byers grinned humorlessly. It consisted merely of a tilting of the corners of his lips. His eyes were still cold and unfriendly. "We're not sure. Yet. Before we can be we want to have a look at that package you're holding for Hong."

"Hong?"

"Don't play dumb, Liddell. We know the old man was in here this morning. We know he left something. We want to see it."

"Oh, him? I didn't recognize the name the way you pronounced it." Liddell grinned. "What's so important about this package?"

"You'll hear all about it if it's what we think it is."

"And if it isn't?" Liddell asked.

"It'll be returned to you intact. Your client will never know it left your hands."

Liddell shrugged. "I guess it's okay."

"It's got to be," the hard-eyed man informed him.

"Suppose I say I can't turn it over without my client's permission?" Liddell countered.

"That would be too bad," there was a new, hard note in the T-man's voice. "In that case we'd have to conclude that you know what's in that package and that you're in cahoots with Hong." He scratched at his eyebrow, studied Liddell through his fingers. "That would be a bad way to get your agency started, Liddell."

"Okay. You talked me into it." Liddell walked around the desk, waited for Byers to get out of the chair, lifted out the package, dropped it on the desk. "That it?"

"You tell me, Liddell."

"That's it," Liddell growled.

The T-man picked it up, studied the seals.

"How about the seals?" Liddell asked. "He'll spot the fact that they've been broken."

"Let us worry about that," Byers told him. He slipped the package into his side pocket. "You won't regret co-operating with us, Liddell."

"You mean I had a choice?" Liddell grunted. He dropped into his chair, glowered at the hard-eyed man.

"No," Byers admitted. "But you could have made us do it the hard way." He perched his hat on the back of his head, signaled for the other two. "We'll let you know about this as soon as we have a look at it," he promised.

Liddell nodded. "Give the girl a receipt on your way out." He watched the group file through the reception room door, swore colorfully under his breath. "Suckered, by God. Suckered by a comic-opera laundryman!"

He reached over, snared the receiver from its hook, dialed a number, tapped impatiently on the desk with stubby fingers. After a moment the phone stopped ringing on the other end; a voice cut in. "Cigar stand."

"Joe? This is Liddell."

"Hello, Mr. Liddell. I've been expecting you to call."

"Did you get the dope I wanted? On the old Chink Pinky put you on this morning?"

The receiver nodded. "Sure thing. It was a breeze. He pulled a hack out of the line out front."

Liddell reached into the humidor, selected a cigar, bit off the end, spat it at the wastebasket. "Know who was pushing it?"

"A regular. Marty Gold."

Liddell scribbled the name on a pad at his elbow. "Is he back on the line yet?"

"I didn't notice. Hold on for a minute and I'll take a look." After a moment his voice returned to the line. "Yeah, he's out there right now. Want me to send him up?"

"No. Tell him to throw his flag. I'll be right down."

"Okay, Mr. Liddell. See you later."

Liddell dropped the receiver back on its hook, walked over to a cabinet built into the far wall. He opened it with a key from his chain, selected a .45 and a shoulder harness from the rack. He slipped out of his jacket, adjusted the harness, checked the .45. Satisfied, he slid it into its hammock, put back his jacket.

The redhead looked up from a typewritten form she was reading. Her make-up stood out like blotches against the pallor of her face; she had been biting on the end of a long, shellacked nail.

"I got the receipt you wanted, Johnny." She held the typewritten sheet out.

Liddell glanced at it, handed it back. "I won't be long. I've got a couple of people I want to see."

"They're not going to make trouble for us, are they, Johnny? We're not responsible for what our clients—" Her eyes widened as she stared at the bulge under his pocket-handkerchief. "You're packing a gun. Why?"

"I like company. Besides, it may come in handy before I get back."

The girl got up from the typewriter desk. "You're not going to start anything, are you, Johnny? Everything's been going so swell. Those federal men are poison. You said so yourself."

"Maybe I'd rather be poisoned than suckered, Pinky."

"The little Chink, you mean? He's not worth getting into a jam over. Leave him to the feds. Let them have him."

Liddell winked. "That's what I intend to do. They're welcome to him. *After* I'm done with him."

CHAPTER TWO

WHEN JOHNNY WALKED UP, Marty Gold, the cabby, was leaning against his left front fender, performing a delicate operation on a molar with the frayed end of a toothpick. He was thin and weazened, and wore a shiny chauffeur's hat so far back on his head that it gave little or no protection to his bald, freckled pate.

"Sorry, chief. I'm taken," he told Liddell, nodding toward the clicking meter. "Waiting for my fare."

"You're Marty Gold, aren't you?" Liddell asked. "I'm your fare. Name's Liddell."

The hackie nodded, leaned back, looked at the meter, smiled benignly. "Hello, partner."

"Let's take a ride," Liddell suggested.

Marty Gold took a last look at the frayed toothpick, flipped it to the sidewalk. "It's your money if you want to go crazy with it." He wrestled with the battered door of the cab, finally got it open. "It ain't the fanciest heap in town, but it'll get you where you want to go."

Liddell got in, leaned back against the cushions. The hackie slid behind the wheel, turned a questioning face toward Liddell. "Where we going?"

"Head downtown," Liddell told him. He winced as the cabby nonchalantly swung the big cab into the rush-hour stream of cabs. Behind him there was a cacophony of screeching brakes and shouted imprecations. The little man at the wheel gave no indication that he heard them.

"Downtown's a big place," he called over his shoulder. "Got any place particular in mind, cap?"

Liddell held his breath for a moment as the driver casually fitted the big car between swaying trucks and lumbering buses with apparent detachment.

"You picked up an old Chink outside the building this morning," Liddell told him. "A little guy. All wrapped up in an overcoat and a hat two sizes too big."

Marty Gold studied him through the rearview mirror. "I remember this character. What about him?"

"I want to know where you took him."

The cabby spotted a hole between two trucks, threw the cab at it, decided at the last minute that he couldn't make it, jammed the brakes on with enough force to skid Liddell halfway off the seat.

"Why?"

Liddell rubbed his knee, scowled at the back of the driver's head. "I want to have a talk with him. I'm a private eye."

"A peeper, huh?" There was a new note of interest in the cabby's voice. "You working for this character or against him?"

"For him, I guess," Liddell growled. "He came into my office, gives me a phony name with a story to match. I figure it might be a good idea to talk it over."

Marty Gold nodded. "I know how you feel. Nothing gives me the burn like getting stiffed myself. I dropped this guy at the corner of Park Row and Worth. Chinatown to you."

Liddell flinched as the cab hurtled out of the line of traffic, squealed into a left turn that made the truck driver coming in the opposite direction stand on his brake.

"Chinatown, eh? That's fine. Now all I've got to do is find a Chinaman in Chinatown," Liddell grunted. "That should be a breeze."

Marty Gold concentrated on his driving for a moment, relaxed at a red light. "Not so tough, maybe. I seen the house he ducked in."

Liddell leaned forward. "You did? Could you point it out to me?"

The light turned green, and the cab lurched forward with a roar, slamming Liddell back against the cushion. "Sure. It's the second from the corner."

"That's some help, at least," Liddell conceded. "Although the way they hole up in those rabbit warrens, it'd take an Act of Congress to locate him."

"I suppose you know this character is heeled?" the cabby put in conversationally. "I make the heater when he opens the coat to pay the tariff on the haul. A very businesslike piece of iron it is, too. Looks like a forty-five from where I sit, which is close enough indeed for me."

The cab jumped a light, scattering a group of pedestrians who screamed their indignation after it.

"I figured he might be," Liddell admitted glumly. "But before I start worrying about that, I better start figuring how I'm going to smoke him out."

Marty swung the cab right on East Broadway, proceeded south. "I got a friend might be able to do you some good in this direction."

"He must be awful good to be able to pick one Chink out of a couple of thousand just from a description."

"It's a her. Goldy LaTour she calls herself. LaTour," he snorted. "She's a LaTour like I'm maybe a Murphy."

"You think she'd be able to pick him out?"

"She can tell them apart in the dark. She's been leading a monkey on a string through Chinatown since I'm a kid on Eldredge Street. And that ain't recent."

"A hustler? What good can she do us? You saw this guy. He was too old to be interested in women. Much too old."

"You sure don't know anything about Chinks, mister," Marty Gold snorted. "Hell, they don't know when they're too old." The cab hurtled off East Broadway under the el structure on Bowery, skidded to a stop at the far side of Worth Street. "I'll park here. Might be a good idea not to park in front of the house and tip this character off. He didn't look like he's packing that rod so's his coat hangs straight."

Liddell leaned forward, studied the old smoke-grimed buildings that lined both sides of the street. He pulled a roll of bills from his pocket, separated a five, passed it up to the driver. "Which house was it?"

The hackie folded the five tenderly, brought his foot up on his seat, slid the bill down the side of his shoe. "In case they shake us down back at the garage," he explained. He squinted out into the street, pointed to an old, rundown stone house. "That one. Second from the corner."

"And this friend of yours? The hustler with the fancy name?"

The cabby nodded. "Her, too. That's where she shacks up. Want me to run in and make with the introduction?"

Liddell grinned. "You're too anxious, Marty. Besides, I don't want you to get mixed up in anything."

"Don't give it a thought. What've I got to lose? A job that's shaking my insides to hell and a wife that starts nagging the minute she wakes up and don't stop until he goes to sleep." He reached down to the floor, came up with a jack handle. "Besides, I might come in handy if things get rough."

Liddell shook his head. "You go on back uptown, Marty. Nothing's going to happen that I can't handle. Me and my client are going to have a little talk and I'm going to resign."

Marty Gold looked disappointed. "That's all?"

"That's all." Liddell got the door open, stood on the curb alongside the cab. "What apartment is this Goldy character in?"

"First floor back." The hackie squinted at him, exposed the brown stubs of his teeth in a grin. "Don't take any drinks on the house. Goldy's a real Mickey Mouse."

"A what?"

"A Mickey Mouse. A mouse what feeds suckers Mickeys. Sets them up for a roll job," Marty explained patiently. "She's a real artist at it, too."

"I'll be careful," Liddell promised.

There were no signs of life in the house as Johnny Liddell walked up the three unwashed steps that led to the foul-smelling vestibule. At some time or other, any number of uninhibited adolescents had made use of its once whitewashed walls to expound sex theories and suggestions in pencil and crayon. Several had taken the trouble to illustrate their works. No one had taken the trouble to obliterate them.

Three rusting tin mailboxes, badly battered, hung askew on one wall. The push buttons in the bells had long since disappeared.

The door to the inner hall stood ajar. Johnny Liddell shouldered it open, walked into the inner hall. An odor compounded of equal parts of unwashed bodies, stale cooking, and inadequate toilet facilities assailed his nostrils. He waited until his eyes had adjusted themselves to the gloom, then peered around. At the far end of the hallway he made out the outline of a door. He felt his way cautiously down the hall, knocked at the door.

After a moment, a whiff of cheap perfume signaled the opening of the door. "Come in, honey. I been waiting for you," a husky voice grated in the gloom. The door creaked open wider, and now Liddell could make out a dark shape silhouetted in the doorway. "Well, come in. I'm not going to hurt you," the husky voice cajoled.

Liddell shrugged, stepped in, heard the door shut behind him, a latch snap.

"We don't want company. An audience makes me nervous," the woman chuckled throatily.

Liddell heard her slippers scudding along the uncarpeted floor, then an unshaded light spilled bright yellow into all but the far corners of the room.

The woman stood by the light, her hand still on the switch. She was tall, big-boned, deep-chested. An old kimono was tied sloppily around her middle, emphasizing her bigness. Her eyes were hard, heavily underlined with makeup, while the rest of her face was blotchy with old, caked powder. Her lipstick was a red, uneven smear across her face, and a mop of brassy-colored hair was piled on top of her head. Her eyes narrowed as she studied Liddell.

"In the wrong pew, ain't you, friend?" the deep voice rasped.

"You're Goldy, aren't you?"

The woman nodded.

"Then you're the one I'm looking for," Liddell told her.

"You're wasting your time, friend." The woman shrugged. "Check in with your inspector. You'll find I'm all paid up on my dues. I got no trouble coming."

Liddell grinned. "I'm not a vice cop. Name's Liddell. I run an agency."

"A peeper, huh? All ways of making a living, I guess." Goldy stared at him for a moment, then shrugged. "Come on in and have a drink. We can talk, anyway." She turned and shuffled toward a closed door at the end of the hall.

Liddell followed her into a small kitchen, took one of the chairs at her invitation. She rummaged in the closet and came up with a bottle and two glasses. She tipped the bottle over each glass, shoved one in front of Liddell.

"It pays to stay friendly with all cops, harness and private. What's on your mind?"

Liddell sniffed at the glass, looked up at the woman. "This stuff okay?"

The woman's laugh was a deep rumble in her throat. "Somebody's been giving away my trade secrets. You don't have to worry about that, friend. I save the other stuff for my paying customers." She lifted her glass to her lips, drained it without a grimace. "Now, suppose you tell me what you're really after."

"A Chink. Calls himself Hong. Small, old, dried up. Face like an old prune. Not a hair on his head. Lives in this house."

Goldy spilled some more liquor in her glass, swirled it around the sides. "That ain't much for a girl to go on." She jabbed at her hair with a red-tipped claw. "What's the beef with this Hong? What do you want him for?"

"No beef. I got something belonging to him I want to give back."

"I might know him," the woman conceded. She emptied her glass, wiped the thick lips with the back of her hand, straddled a chair facing Liddell. "You know, I make my living off these Chinks down here. They could make it awful tough on little Goldy if I was to finger one of them for a bum rap. Besides, I don't like stoolies."

Liddell put down his glass, dug into his pocket for the roll of bills, separated a ten and a twenty, dropped them on the table.

"Put away your money, friend. You're not my type," Goldy told him. She shoved the bills across the table to Liddell.

"There's no grief in it for the old guy," Liddell assured her. "All I want is a few minutes' talk with him, then I bow out."

There was a sharp rapping at the hall door. The woman ignored it, chewed on the stubby end of a crimson nail. The rapping persisted. She swore under her breath, got up, shuffled to the kitchen door. "Go 'way, Charley, I'm busy. You come back later," she yelled.

She shuffled back to her chair, dropped into it. "I wouldn't want to finger anybody for a pinch, you understand. But I might know the guy you're looking for." She picked up her glass, discovered it was empty, slammed it down. "He talk pidgin?"

Liddell shook his head. "Straight American."

Goldy nodded. "Yeah, I know who you mean. He's got a flop upstairs. Second floor back. Right up above here." As Liddell got up from his chair, she caught him by the arm. "Like you said, there'll be no trouble for the old guy?"

Liddell nodded. "No trouble."

The second-floor hallway was even darker and less inviting than the first floor had been. Liddell felt his way carefully, guiding himself along the wall until he came to the door. He knocked softly, slid his hand inside his jacket, loosened the .45 in its holster. There was no sign of anyone answering his knock.

He reached out, rapped his knuckles against the door again. This time when he got no answer he tried the knob. It turned easily in his hand. He pushed the door open, waited. There was a rush of stale air spiced with a smoky, unpleasant smell. Nothing else.

The room beyond was in complete darkness. Liddell stepped inside, closed the door behind him to avoid silhouetting himself as a target for anybody hiding inside. He tugged the .45 from its hammock, transferred it to his left hand.

The hallway was nearly identical to the one in the apartment below. He remembered that the light fixture was halfway down toward the kitchen. Slowly he made his way along the wall, right hand extended, groping for the switch.

There was no sound to indicate the presence of anyone else, but Liddell had the strong sensation that he wasn't alone in the flat. The strong, smoky smell was heavier, and he had the feeling of eyes on him, eyes that could follow his every move despite the pitch-darkness. He stopped, squeezed back against the wall, strained his eyes against the darkness, listened for any sound that might betray another presence. There was no sound but that of heavy breathing. His own.

After a second, he continued to feel for the switch. A few steps farther, he felt it under his fingers. He took a deep breath, flicked it, spilling sudden yellow brilliance into the hallway. At the same moment, he dropped to his knee and brought the .45 into firing position.

Hong, the old Chinese, stood in the doorway to the kitchen, his arms above his head, his long, bony fingers curled like claws. His teeth were bared in a horrible fixed grin, his eyes stared unblinkingly. Two thin wires suspended each of the old man's thumbs to a corner of the doorframe, and the hundreds of wounds and small cigarette burns that dotted the bare chest were mute evidence that his death had been neither quick nor merciful.

CHAPTER THREE

JOHNNY LIDDELL WALKED OVER to the dead man, squeezed past him through the door into the kitchen. It was bare, cold looking, and empty. Tins had been emptied onto the floor; the table drawer had been pulled out, thrown aside.

Another door led into a bedroom beyond. Here, too, there was ample evidence of a relentless search. Drawers had been spilled onto the floor, pillows had been slashed, the unmade bed torn to ribbons. Liddell investigated the other two rooms of the flat, found them empty, equally torn apart.

He stripped the soiled sheet from the bed, walked back to where Hong's body hung in the doorway, and draped the sheet over it, blotting out the dead man's staring eyes, agonized expression.

Back in the bedroom, he stirred the pile of clothing thrown from the drawers with the tip of his shoe. He satisfied himself that whatever the killers had been looking for wasn't pasted to the underside of any drawers. Then he checked the spaces in the bureau behind the drawers, tested the bedposts for concealed hiding-places, lit a match in the upper shelf of the closet, tapped the molding. He found nothing. He had the uncomfortable feeling that the thing the killers had been searching for had, until an hour before, lain carelessly tossed in his own top desk drawer.

He walked back into the outer hall, found a pay phone at the head of the stairs, dialed police headquarters.

"I want to report a murder," he told the bored, metallic voice that had identified itself as "Police headquarters, Sergeant Dolan."

"Give me the location, please," the metallic voice requested.

Liddell gave him the details, promised to stay until the prowl car arrived to take over.

He was on the stoop, finishing a cigarette, when the white-topped police car skidded to a stop out front and two uniformed men spilled out. "You the guy reported a homicide?" the older of the two asked.

Liddell nodded. "Second floor rear." He led the way up to Hong's flat, answered a few routine questions for one cop, while the other prowled aimlessly through the rooms.

"Old guy was probably one of them misers," the younger cop grunted. "Wonder how much he had stashed away. Probably plenty, huh?"

"Let Homicide worry about that," the older cop advised. He finished with Liddell, walked over to the body, lifted the sheet, and studied the wound-covered body. "Old guy sure musta been stubborn." He dropped the sheet back over the body, found a chair, dropped into it with a sigh. "You better hang around until Homicide gets here, mister," he told Liddell. "They might have some questions I didn't think about."

The Homicide detail was headed by Sergeant Mike Crossan, a tall, slow-talking refugee from his native Texas. He nodded to the two uniformed men as he came in, flicked a brief glance at Liddell.

"You find the body?" he asked.

Liddell nodded.

The Homicide man walked over to the dead man, whipped the bed sheet off it, studied the wounds with a practiced eye. Then he indicated for the two men with him to take over. He walked over to the two prowl-car cops, muttered a few words, took the large leather notebook in which the older cop had noted Liddell's answers to his questions. After a moment, he handed the book back, came over to where Liddell was sitting on the edge of the bed.

"Your name's Liddell?" he drawled.

Liddell nodded, made room for the tall man.

Crossan pushed his broad-brimmed fedora on the back of his head, sat down. "I'm Crossan. Sergeant, Homicide," he explained. His eyes roamed around the room, taking in evidences of the search. "Like this when you got here?"

"Haven't touched a thing, sergeant," Liddell told him. "Just tossed a sheet over the old guy. Didn't know how long I'd have to be waiting here looking him in the eye."

The Homicide man nodded, dug a pack of cigarettes from his jacket pocket. "How'd you happen to find him? Live in the building?" He offered the pack to Liddell, then took one himself.

"No. He was a client of mine. I operate a private detective agency."

Crossan held out a light, waited until Liddell had taken a deep drag, expelled a stream of blue-gray smoke. "That's why your name was so familiar. You're the Liddell broke the Murtha jewel case with Inspector Herlehy." He lit his own cigarette, inhaled deeply. "No idea what they were looking for, I suppose?"

"I'm not sure."

"Take a guess," the sergeant invited.

Liddell pinched at his nostrils with thumb and forefinger. "I never saw this guy until this morning. He dropped by my office, paid me a hundred bucks to take care of a package for him."

Crossan raised his eyebrows. "That's a lot of dough just to take care of a package. What was in it?"

Liddell shrugged. "It was sealed."

The Homicide man nodded. "That's probably what they were after. How big is it?"

"About this long by this wide," Liddell illustrated.

"I'll have one of my boys drop by your place and pick it up. That ought to be a big help in cracking this one fast." He signaled to one of the men who had been helping to cut down the body. "Got an errand for you, Cusack."

The plainclothes man nodded, walked over. "What is it, sarge?"

"I want you to pick something up." He turned to Liddell. "Where's your office located, Liddell?"

"The package isn't at my office. Some of the boys from Treasury dropped by with a writ this afternoon and picked it up. They'll probably be glad to give you a report on it." He took a deep drag, let it dribble down his nostrils. "I guess that's all you'll need me for."

The Homicide man nodded. "Not figuring on looking into this on your own?"

"What's there to look into? The old guy had something, dream powder probably, cached it where he thought it would be safe. T-men pick it up and the old guy gets it from his mob. You find out what's in the package, backtrack on the mob, and wrap it up. What's there to look into?"

"That's the nice part of your racket, you can pick and choose," Crossan grunted. "Us, we got to take them as they come." He fished in his pocket for a fountain pen, initialed the disposal form for the medical examiner's man.

"Pretty messy one, eh, sarge?" The white-jacketed intern grinned. "I lean toward the gunshot cases myself. Much cleaner."

Crossan handed back the form, screwed the top back on his fountain pen, jabbed it into his pocket. "What's it look like to you? Tong-war stuff?"

The intern shook his head. "Too crude. Looks more like a Murder Incorporated routine. I drew the chore of burying some of the dead in Jap POW camps after the war. When those Asiatics want information they got better ways of getting it than playing mumbley-peg on your chest with an ice pick. Like that there's too much risk that you'll conk out before you give out with what they want to know."

Crossan dropped his butt to the floor, crushed it out. "I guess so." He got up from the bed, walked to the door with the intern, watched him follow the basket down the narrow stairs.

"Need me any more, sergeant?" Liddell asked. "If you don't, I'd just as soon get back to the office and get some work done."

"Okay. Before you go, give me the name of the agent who picked the stuff up. Foley Square's right on our way. I'll have Cusack drop by and get the report."

"Guy's name was Byers."

Crossan ran the heel of his hand along the side of his jaw, grunted. "Byers, eh? I didn't know he went out in the field any more. Must be important to get the old guy himself out."

"Old guy?" Liddell flipped his cigarette at the sink, scowled. "He's not so old."

"Byers? He's past sixty-five if he's a day."

Liddell investigated the faint stubble of his chin with the tips of his fingers. "Must be two other guys. This Byers was about my height, five ten or eleven, weighed maybe a hundred and ninety or a hundred and ninety-five. Dark hair, square jaw. Around thirty-eight to forty."

Crossan shook his head. "Nothing like the guy I mean. Mine is sixty-five about, short, fat, gray-headed. You sure his name was Byers? Maybe he said he was sent by Byers."

Liddell shook his head. "His name was Byers."

"Must be new in the job. I thought I knew most of the boys in the bureau." He hooked his hand under Liddell's elbow. "Let's go call him and tell him Cusack will be dropping by for the report."

At the phone Crossan gave him the number, Liddell dialed it. A male voice conceded, "This is the federal building."

"Do you have an agent in Treasury named Byers?"

The voice hesitated as though consulting a list. "Yes, sir. He's head of the bureau."

"Is there another Byers? A younger one?"

The voice went back to the list, shook its head. "I only have one Byers listed, sir. Want to talk to him?"

Liddell wiped a thin film of perspiration from his upper lip with the side of his hand. "Put me through."

After a brief pause there was a click of a connection, and a smooth voice came through. "Byers speaking."

"This is Liddell, Byers. Johnny Liddell. It's about that package your office picked up at my office this morning."

"I don't understand. What package?" the smooth voice puzzled.

"What is this?" Liddell growled. "A guy calling himself Byers shoved a writ under my nose this morning and took a package belonging to a client of mine. A man named

Hong. Now Hong's dead and the police want to know what was in that package."

"I'm sure they do," the smooth voice nodded. "But, unfortunately, I don't know what you're talking about. I'm the only Byers in this bureau. I have never been in your office. I know nothing of your client's package. And to the best of my knowledge I have never heard of a man named Hong."

The perspiration was back on Liddell's lip. He returned the receiver to its hook, swore colorfully and encyclopedically under his breath.

"He claims he doesn't know what I'm talking about," Liddell growled to Crossan. "What's he think he's trying to pull?"

"Maybe he doesn't. Maybe the guys that took that package weren't T-men. Maybe they did get what they wanted out of Hong before he conked out."

"You think I'm an amateur? That writ they had was the McCoy. So were Byers's credentials. I've seen enough of them to know the business when I get it."

Crossan looked interested. "I forgot about the writ. Notice who it was issued by?"

"Judge Mason."

The Homicide man consulted his watch, scowled at it. "He'll be out of court by now. Maybe we can catch him at home." He took Liddell's place at the phone, lifted the receiver, dropped a coin, dialed. After a moment, he put his mouth up close to the mouthpiece. "Is the judge in, Mrs. Mason? Sergeant Crossan, Homicide. Yes, ma'am. Very important. If you'll do that, I'll wait here for the call." He squinted at the number stamped on the instrument. "It's Fairview 7-2359. Thank you." He replaced the receiver on its hook. "Mrs. Mason is going to locate him and have him call us here."

Liddell grunted.

"Damn funny," Crossan mused. "You never saw this Hong before he wandered into your office today? Didn't know him?"

Liddell shook his head. "Never laid eyes on him before and I wouldn't lose any sleep if I'd missed him then."

"Wonder how he came to pick you?"

"Don't you read the papers? I'm a famous guy," Liddell growled.

The phone jangled. Crossan scooped it off its hook, held it to his ear. "Crossan here. Hello, Judge Mason. Sorry to bother you at home this way, but it's a murder case. That search warrant you issued today is involved. I'd like to know who asked to have it issued."

The receiver chattered back at him, he wrinkled his brow.

"It was served on Johnny Liddell, a private eye who works pretty close with the department, and—"

The receiver cut him off, chattered metallically. The frown on the Homicide man's face deepened. He nodded mechanically. "I see, judge. Well, thanks very much." He tossed the receiver back on the hook. "Notice the date on that writ, Liddell?" he asked.

"Today's date."

Crossan pursed his lips, balanced back on his heels, his hands laced behind his back. "Judge Mason wasn't in his chambers today. He hasn't been in them since last Monday. He's been taking a complete rest at his doctor's orders. What's more, he says he hasn't signed any search warrants of any kind in several weeks."

Johnny Liddell growled deep in his chest. "Maybe I'm nuts. Maybe the guy isn't dead at all. Maybe he never even came into my office."

Crossan teetered on his heels, stared fixedly at Liddell. "He's dead, all right. That's about the only thing I am sure of," he drawled. "But then, there's no use bothering you about this. You're washing your hands of the whole thing."

"The hell I am," Liddell growled. "Somebody's using me for a patsy, and I don't like it. The old guy was my client and he hired me to take care of a package for him. Okay. Somebody pulled a fast one and waltzed off with the package. I intend to get it back."

The Homicide man grinned bleakly. "It looks as though we're both going the same way. Can I give you a lift?"

"No, thanks. I'll pick up a cab. It might give me a bad name if the neighbors see me riding around in police cars."

CHAPTER FOUR

JOHNNY LIDDELL STEPPED OUT of the slow-moving tide of sightseers, western-garbed Orientals, uninhibited slant-eyed school children screaming the American idiom, and all the other inconsistencies that make Mott Street the Main Street of Chinatown. He branched off into a quiet, almost empty side street where the shops were less garish, substituting dried fish and other Chinese delicacies in their windows for the brightly colored porcelains and garish gimcracks in the tourist traps on Mott. The buildings here were weather-beaten and ancient, but bore their age with dignity. No automobiles rode through the street; the sidewalks were almost empty.

Liddell singled out a house in the center of the block with a large Chinese grocery on its ground floor. The entrance to the dwellings above was a small, unlighted vestibule, its glass door grimy and unwashed. Liddell stopped across the street, looked the building over, seemed satisfied, ambled across to the doorway. A young Chinese, sitting on a soap box outside the grocery, looked up as Liddell stopped in front of the building.

"Looking for someone, mister?" he asked in pure American.

Liddell nodded, gestured toward the second story of the building. "Jimmy Kaiming. On a tong matter."

The Chinese appeared to lose interest. "Kaiming is a hard man to see, mister. Very hard." He looked up from under his lids. "Maybe someone sent you?"

Liddell fished out his wallet, pulled a calling card from an inside compartment. It read:

Eddie Sung
Fancy Chinese Vegetables
218 A Marcy Street
San Francisco, Cal.

Across the face of the card was brush-stroked a series of bold Chinese characters. He handed the card to the Chinese.

The result was electrifying. The man jumped up from the box, bowed slightly. "I did not know, sir, that you came so well recommended. I am sure Kaiming will be pleased to see you." He led the way to the vestibule door, threw it open, fumbled with a section of the molding. The inside door to the hallway clicked open. "At the top of the stairs you will find a door, sir. Just walk in. You will be suitably greeted."

Liddell nodded, replaced the card in his wallet, started up the stairs. At the top of the stairs he found an old wooden door, badly in need of repainting. Whole chunks of paint had peeled off, giving it a mottled appearance. He pushed it open, stepped in.

Four feet beyond was another door, a full-length plate-glass door. As he stepped up to it, there was the buzzing of a circuit breaker and the door swung inward.

The room beyond had apparently once been the whole floor of the building. The walls had been removed to make it a huge meeting room. Its contrast to the exterior of the building was breathtaking.

Priceless carpeting covered the floor from wall to wall, while the walls themselves had been paneled over with cypress. In the center of the room was a long, black, gleaming conference table with rows of intricately carved chairs on either side. At the head of the table was a high-backed throne chair. The lighting in the room was diffused, seemed to come from the walls themselves, although no sign of any fixtures was visible.

As he walked into the room, the huge glass door swung noiselessly shut behind him. He turned to see that from inside the room the door was transparent, although laced with a fine steel mesh. Anyone standing inside the room could see clearly the person seeking admittance.

A frail-looking Chinese girl, wearing the traditional Chinese costume, came up to greet him. There was a doll-like, fragile quality to her as she smiled up at him. "I am Fah Soo, sir. You wish to see Jimmy Kaiming." An elusive accent was still apparent in her speech. "May I know who calls and the nature of your business?"

"The name's Liddell, Fah Soo. Johnny Liddell. I am a friend of Eddie Sung in San Francisco." He fished out the calling card, held it out to her.

She read the card, clasped her hands at her breast, bowed. "I shall tell Mr. Kaiming you are here. Won't you be comfortable?" She indicated a small table and armchairs at the far side of the room.

Liddell walked over, selected a chair, watched the girl disappear through a cleverly disguised door in the paneling. After a moment she reappeared, followed by Jimmy Kaiming.

Kaiming was short, dapper. He wore a carefully taped blue pin-stripe suit; his thick, lustrous black hair was worn in a three-quarter part. He smiled cordially as he walked across the room to Liddell, hand extended.

"I understand we have mutual friends, Mr. Liddell?"

Liddell nodded, shook the extended hand. "Eddie Sung told me that you were the man to see if I ever needed anything here in the East."

Kaiming smiled, sat gracefully in the chair across the table. "I shall try to justify his confidence in me." He clapped his hands, waited until the girl had reached the table. "You will join me in a drink, Liddell?"

"Bourbon if you have it."

Kaiming nodded. "I will join Mr. Liddell in bourbon, Fah Soo." He waited until the girl was out of earshot. "Now, how can I be of service to the friend of my great friend, Eddie Sung?"

"You can help me with my arithmetic." Liddell pulled a pack of cigarettes from his jacket pocket, extended it to the Chinese. "I add up two and two and get nothing. I have the vague feeling that's the wrong answer."

"It concerns Chinatown?" Kaiming took a long jade cigarette holder from his breast pocket, fitted the cigarette to it. "One of my compatriots?"

Liddell nodded. "One of your late compatriots. Little old guy named Hong."

Kaiming looked up. "He is dead?"

"Ice-picked to death a couple of hours ago a few blocks from here."

Without taking his eyes from Liddell's face, Kaiming tilted the cigarette holder from a corner of his mouth, snapped a low flame on a jeweled lighter, touched it to the cigarette. "Ice pick? That is not the method of death of my people, Liddell. Rather it sounds like the stupid sadism of some of your people."

Liddell nodded, watched the girl Fah Soo return to place a tray with two glasses, a bottle of bourbon, and a bowl of ice on the table. "It does sound like a typical gang murder. That being the case, I'll handle that end of it."

"How can I help?" Kaiming asked.

"I want some line on Hong. What racket he might have been mixed up in. Who were his associates, particularly white?"

Kaiming fussed with the geometrically exact points of his pocket-handkerchief. "I cannot help you, Liddell. I know nothing of this Hong or his possible associates or activities. He came here a stranger several months ago. He took no part in tong activities." He leaned over, dumped three pieces of ice into each glass, spilled a sizable slug of bourbon over them.

"Any ideas of what he could have been up to?"

Kaiming straightened up, shrugged. "At best it would only be a guess. But it could be that Hong attempted to muscle into Gee Faw, a practice that could easily become fatal."

"Gee Faw? Gambling, eh?" Liddell reached over, took one of the glasses, tasted it, approved. "How would that fit in with the white angle?"

"The white racketeers have been able to move in and control much of Gee Faw in this territory." A look of irritation momentarily disturbed the Chinese's genial expression. "It has, of course, been through the connivance of some of my compatriots. Perhaps Hong, too, tried to move in with his friends and was eliminated by business competitors." The genial mask slipped back into place. As you know, my compatriots are great gamblers. Fan Tan, Boka Pu, Gee Faw are very important industries in our community."

"And the boys from uptown have moved in on Gee Faw? How about the others?"

Kaiming shook his head. "Only in Gee Faw. Being much like your numbers game, it is most susceptible to police interference. When my compatriots found it necessary to seek protection from the police they sought assistance from more experienced operators." He shrugged. "They have found it more difficult to get rid of the cure than it had been to get rid of the disease. The fixers have kept their foot in."

"Do I know any of these characters with the persistent feet?"

Kaiming shrugged. "You may know one such as Ben Cerla. Through the cupidity of a member of our community, a half-caste named Lee Kung, Cerla has attained much stature in Chinatown. He is a partner with Lee Kung in his gaudy and disreputable *Chinese Heaven*." Kaiming said it as though he didn't like the taste of the words.

Liddell drained his glass, set it back on the table. "Ben Cerla, eh? I remember Ben when he was running most of the protection rackets around town. A nasty little man, if I remember rightly."

The cigarette holder tilted from the corner of the tong leader's mouth. "Your memory is excellent."

"He was one of Hong's associates?"

Kaiming shrugged. "I can only guess. As I told you, I know little of the man Hong and his activities." He took the cigarette holder from his mouth, rolled it between thumb and forefinger. "You are investigating the murder of Hong, Liddell?"

Liddell pinched at his nostrils. "A hundred dollars' worth. Hong came to me on a different matter. He paid me a hundred dollars as a retainer. I expect to give him his hundred dollars' worth."

Kaiming nodded. "Quite honorable. However, we are both aware that a hundred dollars is meager pay for the job that would lay ahead in solving his murder. I would like to retain you to do so."

"Why? You say you hardly know him."

"True. Yet, he was a member of our community, and he was murdered by an outsider. That must not be permitted to happen. I would consider it a favor if you would undertake the assignment in my behalf." Kaiming, got up from his chair, paced a short area near the desk. "If, in your investigation into the murder of Hong, you turn up some evidence that will make it possible for us to free our community from the clutches of outside racketeers, you will not find us ungrateful."

The city room of the *Advance* was almost deserted when Johnny Liddell walked in an hour later. He picked his way through the organized confusion of the desks, acknowledged a few greetings from the handful of shirt sleeved men who sat pecking away at typewriters of various ages and vintages.

Jim Kiely, the crime-reporter-turned-city-editor of the *Advance*, tossed a clipped-up copy of the competitive morning sheet into the barrel-sized wastebasket at his elbow as Liddell came up.

"Hi, Johnny." His sharp gray eyes peered inquisitively. "What's new?"

Liddell shrugged. "Can't prove anything by me, Jim. All I've been doing lately is finding out that one half of a family doesn't know how the other half loves. Or who." He cleared a corner of the desk, perched on it. "Where's Muggsy?"

"On an assignment." Kiely pulled a charred brier from his upper drawer, started packing it with coarse-cut tobacco. His eyes never left Liddell. "She'll be back at about nine-thirty if something's cooking. You got something?"

Liddell shrugged. "I don't know. Get anything on that killing down in Chinatown this afternoon? Little Chink named Hong."

"A killing?" Kiely screwed his brow in concentration. "Don't remember anything offhand. Wait, I'll check rewrite." He spun in his swivel chair, yelled to one of the shirt-sleeved men pounding away at a typewriter. "Hey, Roddy! Anything in the stuff from Mac down at the Elizabeth Street station house?"

The rewrite man looked up, peered nearsightedly at a pile of copy paper in his basket. "Nothing much. Couple of gambling raids, a Chink found dead in a tenement—"

"That's the one," Liddell told Kiely.

"What've you got on the dead Chink?"

The rewrite man picked up the copy paper, glanced through it, shrugged. "The usual. Sounds like he welshed on a bet or something, so they cut him up as a lesson to other welshers." He frowned at a penciled notation in the corner of the sheet. "News desk wants me to hold it to a stick."

Kiely nodded, swung back to Liddell. "That the one?" He looked disappointed. "For a minute I thought you had something we could blow up into a story." The sharp eyes studied Liddell's face. "How come you're interested in it?"

"The dead guy was a client of mine."

The city editor scratched a wooden match on the underside of the desk, held it to the pipe. He sucked noisily for a moment, finally got it going. "What would a guy like that want a private eye for?"

Liddell shrugged. "Something big enough to make a couple of guys make like T-men, forge a writ, and snatch it right from under my nose."

"Snatch what?"

"Who knows? It was sealed in a package that Hong left with me."

Kiely sucked thoughtfully on his pipe. "Make like T-men, eh? That means white men."

"Yeah. Matter of fact, it's beginning to look like our Mr. Hong was playing footsy with an old buddy of yours. Ben Cerla."

Kiely grunted. "That's cozy. That means Hong could have been mixed up in anything. Cerla never did care how low he'd have to stoop to pick up a dirty dollar." He leaned back, hooked his heel on the corner of his desk. "If Cerla shows in this job, Johnny, you're a sucker to stick your neck out unless there's plenty in it."

"It's no charity pitch, Jim," Liddell assured him. "I've got me a client. Jimmy Kaiming of the tong."

The city editor's eyebrows rose. "Kaiming, eh? Say, there could be a yarn in this, after all. Why should a guy like Kaiming pay good money to find the killer of a two-bit racketeer? The police will handle it for nothing."

Liddell snorted. "Sure they'll handle it. For how long? The guy's just a nobody who got himself knocked off. Tomorrow there'll be another one and this one will be filed for future reference. The files are full of floaters and nobodies who bowed out with an obituary that says 'Unsolved.' Take a look at how you're handling it. A paragraph or two."

"That's all it's worth," Kiely argued. "Like you say, there's a floater or a bum gets knocked off every day. One more or less don't mean a thing. That is, unless you can dig up something to make this one more important than the rest." He looked hopefully at Liddell. "Think I you can?"

"I might if I get any kind of a break. Right now I don't even have a lead. I don't even know what the hell was in the package," Liddell growled. "Yet, that's apparently the key to the whole mess. That's what he was killed for. They tortured him until he told them where it was, then they came and got it."

"You'd know them if you saw them?"

"Damn right I would. I was wondering if there was anything in your files would help. Any pictures of Cerla's old mob. Something like that?"

Kiely considered it, nodded. "Might find something. Want an authorization to go through it?"

Liddell shook his head. "Haven't got the time. I haven't even checked back to my office. How about having Muggsy go through the Cerla file and picking out anything that might help?"

"You going to see her tonight?"

"I tried to reach her at home to set it up but there's no answer. Ask her to meet me at Luigi's at about ten, will you, Jim?"

Kiely nodded. "I hope you're onto something, Johnny. The kid can use a good break like you gave her on the Raymond killing. She sure looked good on that one."

"I thought you wanted to discourage her. You're always yelling that newspaper work for women is a fate worse than death, you old fake."

Kiely grinned. "We don't let the relatives know what she's doing. They think she's working for Polly Adler." His eyes roved up to the big clock over his desk. He sighed. "I'm going to have to kick you out, shamus. We're about to go to work."

Liddell nodded. "I can take a hint. Just let me check my answering service, will you?" He picked up a phone from the corner of the desk, dialed his office number, waited. After a moment, a voice responded.

"This is Liddell. Any calls for me?"

There was a slight pause, then: "Your secretary has been trying to reach you all afternoon. She wants you to call her at home the minute you check in. No other calls."

Liddell nodded, depressed the bar on the phone, dialed another number. The office redhead's worried voice came through. "That you, Johnny? I've been trying to reach you all evening. Where you been?"

"Out drumming up trade. What's up?"

"The office. Somebody broke into the office, smashed it all to hell. They broke into the desk, the files, everything. It's wrecked."

Liddell rubbed the heel of his hand along his chin, swore. "When did this happen, Pinky?"

"I'm not sure. When you didn't come back, I left about four-thirty. About six-thirty Mike, the elevator boy, called me here at home. He saw a light in the office, thought I was there, and went in to say hello. Somebody hit him over the head."

"Have you been down there since?"

"Who, me?" the phone wailed. "You're the detective, not me. I don't get paid to have permanent waves put in my skull."

"Okay, okay. I'll be in touch as soon as I have a chance to get down there and see what damage has been done." He slammed the receiver back on its hook.

"What's up, Johnny?" Kiely wanted to know.

"I don't know. Somebody went through my office and tore hell out of it looking for something."

"The package?"

Liddell nodded. "Must be. That means whoever killed Hong didn't know the other gang picked it up. Then who the hell was the mob that posed as T-men?"

Kiely surrounded himself with a blue-gray fog of smoke. "It means something else, Johnny. It means the killers don't know the other mob got the package, so they think you've got it. They'll be coming for you next. You sure you don't know what was in that package?"

"No. But, by God, I intend to find out."

Kiely's eyes wandered up to the clock. "Let me know when you do. Right now, I got work to do. I'll tell the kid to meet you at Luigi's at ten. If she can't make it, she can call you there."

Liddell nodded, started back through the welter of desks' that had suddenly become peopled with shirt-sleeved men and women still wearing their hats. An army of boys, armed with galley proofs and copy, darted in and out of lanes in response to a yell of "Copy." Typewriters were beginning to chatter metallically, the sharp tinkling of a bell punctuating the incessant patter of the keys.

The early edition of the *Advance* was getting ready to go to bed.

CHAPTER FIVE

THE CAB DROPPED Johnny Liddell in front of an old brownstone house in what appeared to be a strictly residential section of Brooklyn. There was no indication of a restaurant other than the oversized garbage can out front.

Liddell tossed the cabby a bill, walked to the basement door, rang the bell next to the iron grillwork of the door. After a moment, the inside wooden door opened, silhouetting a huge woman who waddled slowly to the entrance.

"Is Mr. Liddell." She smiled her welcome. "Come in, come in. Is long time since you pay Luigi and Seraphine a visit."

Liddell walked past her into the dining room. The walls had been broken out of what was apparently once a basement apartment to make one huge room. In the far corner, an old-fashioned wood-burning stove encouraged a few pots to give off a tantalizingly spicy aroma. There were only two other customers lingering over coffee at the red-checked-clothed tables. Liddell selected a table across the room from them.

"Miss Ronny, she call for you," the fat woman puffed to Liddell. "She say for you to wait. She may be little late."

Liddell nodded.

"Maybe a little wine while you waiting? Nice Chianti just like you like?" A slight mustache added brilliance to her toothy smile. "What you say?"

"Sounds good, Seraphine," Liddell assured her. He watched her waddle to the cabinet near the stove, return with a fiber-covered bottle and two glasses.

"You wait until Miss Ronny come before you eat, no?"

Liddell nodded. Seraphine gave him another flash of her smile, waddled over to the table of the other customers. Liddell poured himself a glass of the wine and settled back to wait. After a few minutes the other couple left, leaving the entire dining room to him. He was on his third glass of wine when Muggsy walked in the door.

She was wearing a long, loose fitting coat that hung from the shoulders. Her long blond hair was caught in a soft, bun at the nape of her neck. She waved to Seraphine, who was conducting some secret rite with the pots at the stove, and walked over to Liddell.

"Hope you haven't been waiting too long, Johnny. I got tied up at the office." She bent over him, covered his lips with her soft ones. "You needn't look so cross. It's only a few minutes past ten."

"That should be my biggest headache, baby." He helped her out of her coat, draped it over the back of a chair. "I'm not looking cross, I'm concentrating. Making like a detective."

"Been having a bad time, I hear." She sank into her chair with a sigh. "How's the office?"

Liddell poured some wine into her glass, slid it over to her. "All torn to hell. Filing cabinets smashed, desk busted open. Wrecked." He scowled at his glass. "To coin a phrase, you wouldn't know the old place."

"That's a tough break," Muggsy sympathized. "Any idea of who might be behind it?"

Liddell indicated the Manila envelope she had deposited on the corner of the table. "Not yet. But I hope you may have a clue for me in there." He waited while Seraphine came over, ran par for the course in fussing over Muggsy, then retired to the stove to dish out two steaming plates full of the blonde's favorite dish. Find anything worthwhile in the Cerla file?"

"I don't know what you call worthwhile, but from what I did find I gather your playmate Cerla is a real icy character. He doesn't sound to me like the kind of a guy to play games with."

Liddell reached for the envelope, Muggsy snatched it out of reach. "Just a minute, chum. Before you get to this we've got some terms to make," she reminded him. "What's my angle if this stuff tells you what you want to know?"

"What do you want, Shylock?"

"The whole story. Exclusive."

Liddell grinned. "Of course you get it. After all, your father's one of my best friends, isn't he?"

Muggsy grinned back. "You know, sometimes I don't know who to be the most worried about with you—my father or that Lydia Pinkham blonde you play footsy with up in your office. Have you found out if she can type yet?"

"You mean secretaries are supposed to do that, too?" Liddell retorted, and pulled the Manila envelope out of her hand.

Muggsy's effort to grab the envelope back was thwarted by the return of Seraphine with two brimming plates of spaghetti and veal and peppers. The blonde took a deep breath. "God help the diet tonight, she murmured.

Liddell glanced at her profile in the sweater. "You can't get too much of a good thing." He sampled the dish in front of him, burned his tongue, swore under his breath. "Look out for that stuff, it's red-hot."

"Well, while it's cooling off, suppose you tell me what this case is all about. Where does Cerla fit into it?"

"I'll tell you after you eat," Liddell told her, and she had to be satisfied with that. After both plates were cleaned and a grinning Seraphine had collected them, Liddell leaned back, lit two cigarettes, passed one to the blonde.

"Now stop stalling and give out with the details," she insisted.

"That's something I don't have too much of," Liddell growled. "An old Chinaman named Hong left a package with me for safekeeping. A couple of hours later three guys come in, flash Treasury identification and a search warrant, pick up the package."

"Why? What was supposed to be in it?"

Liddell shrugged. "They told me they'd let me know after the bureau had looked it over. It was a sucker play on my part, of course, but I was so mad at the old guy for passing a hot potato over to me, I didn't put up any squawk."

"Where does Cerla fit in?" Muggsy wanted to know.

"I'm not sure he does. Your old man probably told you the Chink was found dead—tortured to death, as a matter of fact—and that Jimmy Kaiming of the tong is footing the bill to get the killer." He poured a half glass of wine into each of the glasses, sipped at his. "Kaiming thinks Hong was mixed up with Cerla. He thinks they were trying to muscle into the local gambling combine."

Muggsy swirled her wine around in her glass, frowned. "If they got the package by posing as T-men, why did they come back and bust up your office?"

"Who knows?" Liddell growled in exasperation. "I had it figured that the killers tortured Hong, made him tell where the package was, then came up to my office and picked it up. Now I'm not so sure. Now I think the killers probably came up and tore the place apart looking for it."

"Then they may think you still have it?" Muggsy asked. "That's cozy. Suppose they come looking for it again?"

Liddell shrugged. "If I find what I'm looking for in this envelope, maybe I'll have it back by then and be waiting for them." He picked up the Manila envelope, undid the metal clasp, dumped a pile of clippings on the table. "I had a good look at the guys who posed as T-men. If they were Cerla's boys, chances are they've been mugged with him at one time or another."

Clipping by clipping, Liddell traced Ben Cerla's career from a petty bootlegger to protection czar of most of New York's vice. Three murder indictments had failed to produce a conviction; various other charges of corruption and racketeering were likewise unproven.

"Nice character you're going up against, Johnny," Muggsy shuddered. "Looks like he has all the protection in the world sewed up, and—" She broke off, frowned at a yellowed clipping Liddell was studying. "Let me see that one a minute, Johnny." She held it under the light, frowned at it for a moment. "Well, what do you know?"

Liddell leaned over, looked at the picture of three men she was holding. "Find something?"

Muggsy indicated a thin, dapper man in the center of the trio. "That fellow right there," she picked him out with a long, carefully shellacked fingernail, "is Runt Brin. Until this very minute I never knew Brin was mixed up in that charity gambling swindle nine or ten years ago. What do you know?"

Liddell took the clipping, read it. "What's more interesting is that he was mixed up with Cerla. The two of them and another guy named Newkirk rigged a fake charity affair, set up crooked roulette wheels, and took the crowd for plenty. Any follow-ups on this one?" They rummaged through the pile of clippings, came up with a handful, set about reading them carefully. "All three indicted. Newkirk decides to turn state's evidence, caught a bad case of lead poisoning in a parked car one night. Indictment squashed." He tossed down the clippings. "What about this Hunt Brin character, Muggsy?"

"Just another café-society character. Seems to be well heeled with money, floats around with a fast crowd." She bit on the end of a shellacked nail. "Funny I never heard about this caper."

Liddell consulted the date on the clip. "Happened before the war. People forget awful fast. Besides, this café-society mob is made up of a lot of people who made their money during the war, and most of them can't afford to throw any stones about where other people get their money." He crushed out his cigarette in the metal tray on the table, drained his glass. "Come across any reference to this Lee Kung yet? He's Cerla's partner in the Chinese Heaven."

"Not by name." Muggsy sorted through the pile of clippings, came up with a batch clipped together. "Here's a series of feature articles Ed Blesch did for the paper on racketeering in New York, where he mentions Ben Cerla as top man in organized vice. Says he has representatives in little Italy, Chinatown, Yorkville and San Juan Hill—all watching his interests. I figure that Chinatown rep might be Kung."

Liddell nodded, took the clips, skimmed through them.

The peal of the doorbell failed to register with either of them. They were both immersed in the clippings when

Seraphine, muttering under her breath, shuffled to the door.

It was her scream that brought Liddell to his feet. Actually, it wasn't much of a scream, didn't get much beyond the first high note. As Liddell jumped up, he saw the fat woman's knees buckle, her huge weight crash to the floor. He had a glimpse of three figures in the doorway, guns in hand.

Liddell's hand streaked for the .45 in his shoulder holster. It froze, fingers brushing the gun butt, at a yelled command from the nearest of the three men.

"Don't try anything, Liddell," the gunman ordered. A .38 special, its sawed-off snout pointing at Liddell's belly, backed up the command.

The gunman stepped out of the vestibule into the candlelight, walked over to where Liddell stood, spun him around, fanned him expertly. He relieved him of the .45, tossed it to the far corner of the room. "Just keep looking at the wall and keep the hands where I can see them, or both you and the girl get it."

Liddell heard other footsteps behind him, then Muggsy gasped indignantly. He started to swing around, when the first blow landed. It sounded like an explosion in his ears, drove him to his knees.

Somewhere, far away, somebody screamed, and the scream seemed to hang on the air in front of his eyes. He tried to struggle to his feet when the dull noise boomed in his ear again. This time there was no pain, just the dull boom in his ears. He had the feeling that the wall was tilting over on him, tried to get out of its way. Although his eyes were open, a dull-red haze swirled in front of them, blocking out all view.

He managed to get out of the way, tried painfully to get on his hands and knees. The toe of a shoe caught him on the side of the jaw, slammed him against the wall.

He lay still.

Consciousness seared its way slowly and painfully into Johnny Liddell's brain. He tried to raise his head, groaned, let it fall back. Dimly he could hear a voice crooning to him.

"Johnny! Johnny, are you all right?"

The familiar voice jangled on hypersensitive nerves. He tried to nod his head, regretted the impulse. He experimented with raising his eyelids, found it only introduced a blinding white light to the inside of his skull. A cool hand was massaging the sore spot on the side of his jaw.

He tried opening his eyes again, and after a moment they stopped rolling back in his head long enough for him to identify the hand as Muggsy's and to discover that he was lying with his head in her lap. She tried a weak smile on him.

"Say, you trying to scare me to death? I didn't think you were ever going to open your eyes." The worried lines around her eyes belied the lightness of her tone. "I should have known they couldn't kill a detective by hitting him on the head."

Liddell tried to sit up, found the room spinning, sank back. He fought back nausea, closed his eyes for a second.

"Just lie quiet for a second, Johnny," Muggsy told him. "The doctor is taking care of Seraphine. He'll be right here."

"I don't need a doctor," Liddell muttered. "All I need is my forty-five and a chance at those guys in an alley. Did you get a good look at them?"

"One of them," Muggsy told him. "The one that slugged you. I'll know him the next time I see him."

"Good," Liddell groaned. "He's the one I want to have a talk with." He opened his eyes slowly, found that he could sit up. He touched the sore spot on the top of his head gingerly. "Is Seraphine all right?"

Muggsy nodded. "More scared than hurt, I think. She's got a bump on the top of her head, but I don't think it's serious. They took her up to her room." She helped him to his feet, waited while he steadied himself on the back of a chair. "You all right, Johnny?"

Liddell nodded, regretted it vocally. "How about you, Muggsy? They rough you up, too?"

"I'm all right. You were the one they wanted." She lit a cigarette, held it to his lips. "They took you apart, looking for something. It sounded to me like they thought you might have a package-room receipt or baggage check." She indicated the clippings strewn all over the floor. "It wasn't the clips. They hardly looked at them."

Liddell inhaled deeply, blew the smoke through his nostrils. "It's that damn package again."

"Not the ones that posed as the T-men?"

"No. This must be the other gang. The ones that busted up the office. They must have been waiting for me, tailed me here." He winced as he massaged the sensitive spot on the side of his jaw. "Looks like they're not going to give up until they get it."

Overhead, heavy footsteps pounded. Liddell grimaced, held his head. A pair of blue-clad legs came into sight on the stairway leading down from the living-quarters above.

"Let me handle this, Muggsy," Liddell whispered.

A young patrolman came over to where they stood. He whipped a large leather notebook from his hip pocket. "Feel up to answering a few questions, folks?" He looked Liddell over sympathetically. "You feel okay, mister? The doc'll be down in a few minutes. The old gal's been kicking up some."

"I'm okay. I don't need the doc," Liddell told him.

The patrolman shrugged, consulted his notebook. "Looks like a stick-up that didn't come off, far as I can see. The old gal says she's not missing anything. How about you?"

Liddell went through the motions of patting his pockets, shook his head. "Looks like everything's here. Must've gotten scared off before they could get anything." He took a deep drag, stubbed out the cigarette. "Amateurs, probably."

The cop nodded, scribbled laboriously in his notebook, took down their names and addresses. "If you want to wait around, I'll send the doc down to have a look at that head of yours."

"No, thanks. I'm all right," Liddell insisted.

"Suit yourself." The cop touched the peak of his cap in a salute to Muggsy, went back up the stairs. As soon as his legs had disappeared in the stairwell, Liddell picked up his hat, brushed himself off. "Let's get this stuff together and get out of here before he gets back. We've got places to go."

Muggsy let him help her into her coat, scooped the clippings up from the floor, dumped them back in the envelope while Liddell returned his belongings to his pockets.

"For once in your life you're right. You have got places to go. Bed. You're going home to bed. My home."

Liddell forced a grin. "How you do talk. Inviting a man home to your house to bed. What would your father say?"

Muggsy grinned. "Let my father talk for himself." The grin faded when Liddell winced putting his hat on. "Seriously, Johnny, I think my place is safest tonight. They've been to your office, they followed you here. The next place they'll try is your apartment. And you're in no condition to handle them."

"But I haven't got the time to go to bed. I've got to get these guys, Muggsy," Liddell protested. "You saw them. You can probably pick them out at Identification and we can get started. Now we've got something to go on."

Muggsy nodded. "You'll have all day tomorrow for that. I'll go down to headquarters with you the first thing in the morning. But tonight we're going home and take care of that skull of yours!"

CHAPTER SIX

THE FOLLOWING MORNING, Johnny Liddell and Muggsy Kiely were at Centre Street, asking for Inspector Herlehy. The sergeant at the desk shook his head doubtfully at their prospects for getting in, was prevailed upon to check his hunch with a phone call, reversed himself.

"The inspector says for you to go right up," he said. Inspector Herlehy sat slumped behind the battered old desk in his cubbyhole office. He waved to them as they came through the door, motioned them into the old-fashioned wooden armchairs across the desk from him.

"Looks like crime is picking up, with you two working in harness again," he greeted them. "What's on your minds?"

"As though you didn't know," Liddell growled. Herlehy grinned. "I have been hearing some things about you, at that." He reached over, picked up a typewritten flimsy from the tray on the corner of his desk. "Liddell appears on two reports turned in during the past twenty-four hours. Found a body in Chinatown, was a witness to a stick-up in Brooklyn. Busy little fellow, aren't you?" The inspector rolled his eyes upward, regarded Liddell questioningly. He chewed placidly on his customary wad of gum. "Decide to take us into your confidence?"

"We could use some help," Liddell conceded.

Herlehy shifted to a more comfortable position on his hard wood seat. "Do tell."

"All right to smoke?" Liddell asked. The inspector nodded, watched without comment while Liddell and the girl lit up. "What do you want to know?" Liddell asked him.

"Take me from the beginning," Herlehy suggested.

"You got Crossan's report, so you know all about the package Hong left with me and the phony T-men who picked it up." Herlehy nodded, didn't interrupt. "I had no intention of working on the Hong murder until they pulled that. Well, now I'm on the case with both feet. The agency has been retained by Jimmy Kaiming to get the killer."

Herlehy raised his eyebrows, didn't miss a beat on his gum.

"Kaiming thinks Ben Cerla may be mixed up in the killing."

"Why?" Herlehy wanted to know.

Liddell shrugged. "A hunch, I guess. He figures Hong was trying to muscle into the Gee Faw racket in Chinatown, maybe stepped on Cerla's toes or maybe crossed him."

Herlehy nodded for him to go on.

"I had a look at the fake T-men who got the package. I figured they might be some of Cerla's men, so I had Muggs dig up the *Advance* file on Cerla and his mob."

"Find anything?"

Liddell shook his head. "Nothing much. While we were going through it, three guns busted into Luigi's and stuck us up. Muggsy got a good look at the head man and thinks she may be able to pick him out of the files in Identification."

Herlehy shifted the wad of gum from one side of his mouth to the other. "Could be. But first, what were they after, Liddell?"

"I don't know, inspector. That's the truth. My guess is they thought I had the package."

Herlehy scowled. "You just told me they got the package by posing as Treasury men."

"There must be two mobs after it. That's the only way it makes sense to me."

"What's so important about this package, Liddell?"

Liddell shrugged, grinned bleakly. "That's one of the things I expect the guy Muggsy's going to identify to tell us."

"If he's on file," Herlehy grunted. He jabbed at the buzzer on his desk, waited until a uniformed patrolman stuck his head in the door. "Had breakfast, you two?"

"Cooked it with my own lily-white hands," Muggsy boasted. "But I could stand some coffee."

Herlehy nodded. "You, Liddell?"

"Black."

"Three coffees, Ray. Rush them up, will you?" After the door had closed behind the young cop, Herlehy leaned across the desk toward Liddell. "This dead guy. What do you know about him?"

"Not a thing. He just walked into my office from nowhere, hired me to take care of his package, and walked out."

"How about Jimmy Kaiming? He know anything about him?"

Liddell shook his head. "Nothing worth while. Hong kept pretty much to himself. How about you? You been able to dig up anything?"

"Sent his prints to Washington. Nothing yet." Herlehy leaned back, stared up at the ceiling. "Far's we've been able to find out, no one knew him when he was alive and nobody wants to know anything about him now that he's dead. Still, somebody must have known him pretty well to do the job on him they did."

"Have you tried the Coast? When he came into my office, the first thing he asked me was if I was the Johnny Liddell who worked on the Randolph deal out there nine or ten years back. I figured he might be a Coaster come East. Maybe a line to the L.A. and Frisco police might turn up something."

Herlehy indicated a yellow telegraph form in his basket. "Crossan mentioned that in his report. We teletyped out there. Not a thing on him on file." He scowled, ran his palm over the silver bristles on his chin. "Looks like he just popped out of nowhere long enough to get himself killed in my territory."

"How come you're so interested in this stiff, inspector? He's just another floater."

"That's right," Herlehy grunted. "I'm just keeping an eye on it to find out why you're so interested."

There was a light tap on the door, the uniformed patrolman came in, deposited two containers on the desk, handed one to Muggsy. "The one on the left is black," he told Liddell.

The inspector waited until the door had closed behind the cop, reached over, took one of the containers, gouged the top out of it. "Besides, I'm curious to get a look at this famous package. The one that nobody but you seems to have seen."

"You'll get a look at it. As soon as I lay my hands on the mob that hijacked it," Liddell promised. "And the only way I'm going to be able to do that is if you string along on this identification."

Herlehy nodded, swirled the coffee around the inside of the container. "Suppose by some freak chance Muggsy does make one of these guns in Identification section. Naturally, you're going to turn him over to us to handle?"

"Naturally," Liddell lied blandly.

Herlehy grinned, took a sip of the coffee, then stirred it with a finger. "You're a cockeyed liar. What are you really going to do if you catch up with these guys?"

Liddell shrugged. "Just have a little talk with them."

"Suppose they don't talk?"

Liddell picked up his container of coffee, cupped his hands around it, smiled frostily. "Want to bet?"

Herlehy sighed, shrugged. "I don't suppose it would be any use to try to convince you it'd be a lot smarter to let us handle him?"

"Maybe you don't know the right questions," Liddell countered.

"Or the right way to ask them?"

Liddell shrugged. "Could be."

Herlehy turned to the girl. "You really think you'd recognize this guy if you saw him again, Muggsy?"

She nodded. "I'd know the leader, all right. He was the one that slugged Johnny. I'll know him if I see him again."

Herlehy tapped on the edge of the desk with stubby fingers, finally nodded. "Okay, let's go down to Identification and see how good that memory of yours really is." He swung back to Liddell. "But let's you and me understand each other, Liddell. I'm going to play ball with you on this one. But that doesn't mean I'm giving you a hunting-license. If you get to this guy before we do, I want to hear about it. While he's still alive!"

Liddell nodded. "It's a deal, inspector."

Herlehy drained his container, crushed it into a ball, tossed it at the wastebasket. "Maybe I'm sticking my neck out, but I've got a funny feeling that there's a lot more to this one than appears on the surface. This isn't just the murder of a floater. And maybe a guy like you with a personal stake in it, and not tied hand and foot by regulations, can make some sense out of it."

"I intend to," Liddell grunted.

"Okay. Maybe you will and maybe you won't. Maybe you'll make me and the department look awful smart, and maybe you'll just make room for me with you behind the eight ball. I'll take the chance. But I'll expect you to level with me all the way."

Liddell nodded.

Herlehy got up from behind the desk. "All right. As long as we all understand each other, let's get the show on the road."

He led Liddell and the girl down a long corridor, lined with frosted-glass doors, turned at a sharp right angle, brought up at a door labeled *Identification Section.* Herlehy opened the door, led the way in.

The room was huge, lined on three sides with mammoth filing cabinets. In the center of the room, under large overhead lights, were two long library-type tables. A man wearing a lieutenant's badge pinned to his blue serge suit sat at a small oak desk near the poor, riffling through a stack of filing cards. He looked up, smiled at Herlehy.

"Hi, inspector. You don't get back here very often these days." He looked from Herlehy to Liddell and the girl, back to Herlehy. "Going to do some fishing?"

"Yeah, Martin. This is Ronny Kiely of the *Advance* and Johnny Liddell, a private eye. Miss Kiely thinks she can identify one of your boarders. Lieutenant Martin is in charge down here, Muggsy," he added.

"You think your man has gone through our fishbowl, eh, Miss Kiely?" the lieutenant asked. "If he has, we'll find him for you." He drew a large Manila pad in front of him. "Suppose you tell me something about him. That may make it easier."

Muggsy looked to Liddell for help. "Where do I start?"

"Well, I got a few fleeting impressions of him that might help," Liddell volunteered. "He's a gunman, I think he probably puts his gun up for hire. He must be about my height, a right-hander." He felt the tender spot on his head.

The lieutenant took some notes. "That's all you saw of him?"

"I didn't have much of a chance. He was behind me most of the time. Miss Kiely got a better look at him."

"How about it, Miss Kiely?" the lieutenant asked patiently.

"Like Johnny says, he was about his height. A lot lighter, though. I—I think his hair was black. From the way he talked, he might be an Italian or a Greek."

The lieutenant nodded, made some notes. "How about any peculiarities in the way he walked or talked? Any deformities, marks of any kind?" he asked.

Muggsy started to shake her head, stopped. "Do you mean skin blemishes? Things like that?"

"Anything at all. The way he parted his hair, whether he wore glasses or jewelry. Acne. Birthmarks. Anything."

"I don't know about his hair. He was wearing a hat, but I did notice some kind of a mark under his right ear. Sort of like a large freckle."

"Nothing else?" the Identification man asked.

Muggsy caught her lower lip between her teeth, contracted, finally shook her head. "That's all I remember. But if I saw him, I'd know him."

The lieutenant nodded again, finished his notes. "We'll get you some pictures to look at, Miss Kiely." He got up from behind the desk, walked over to a library table, pulled out a chair for her. Liddell and Herlehy found chairs next to her.

"I'll be right back," the lieutenant promised. He disappeared through the corridor door, return in a few minutes with two patrolmen. They immediately busied themselves at the huge files, started bringing drawers of classified pictures to set in front of the girl.

The lieutenant returned to his desk, busied himself with his filing cards. Liddell and Herlehy leaned back in their chairs, watched Muggsy study picture after picture. Several hours later, she stopped at a picture, chewed on the end of her fingernail.

"Got him?" Liddell asked.

"I—I don't know. I think this looks like him."

Herlehy stood in back of the girl's chair, looked over her shoulder. "'Lunfaro, Dominick,'" he read. He looked up at Liddell. "How about it, Johnny? He look familiar to you?"

Liddell stared at the hard face in the file, scowled in concentration, finally shook his head. "I didn't get a good enough look at him. It could be."

"Let's get the rundown on him," Herlehy suggested. He lifted the card out of the file, turned it over. "Five feet ten, sallow complexion, about a hundred and sixty pounds, dark hair, brown eyes. Scar in upper left quadrant, knife scar on right arm, brown skin blemishes prominent body and right jaw." He looked up. "Sounds like him."

"I'm almost sure it is, inspector," Muggsy told him wearily. "It's just that after you've looked at so many pictures they all begin to look alike."

Herlehy nodded. "Here's something for you, Liddell," he referred back to the card. "Known narcotic addiction. Dangerous." He replaced the card in the file. "What do you think?"

Liddell jotted the name down on the back of an envelope. "I think it mightn't be a bad idea to have a talk with him."

"I didn't mean that. He's a known hophead and killer."

"So what?"

Herlehy shrugged. "Lunfaro, Ben Cerla. This deal doesn't sound like the kind a guy should go up against alone. Why don't you sit tight until we flush Lunfaro out for you, Liddell?"

"I think I can do the job quicker."

Herlehy grunted. "How can you do a job like this quicker than eighteen thousand trained men?"

"They've got other things on their mind. Me, there's only one thing I'm interested in. Finding him. Believe me, inspector, I'll do the job quicker."

Herlehy shrugged, thanked the lieutenant in charge, led the way back to his office. He walked over to the window, stared down into the street below.

"I can't stop you from trying to crack this thing by yourself, Liddell. All I can do is tell you to be careful. These boys play for keeps."

Liddell nodded. "So do I."

Herlehy turned from the window, walked back to his desk, "I'll help you all I can, but that doesn't mean that I won't bear down hard if you get trigger-happy. We understand each other?"

"We understand each other," Liddell told him. He consulted his watch, grunted. "I'd better get on the bicycle, inspector. I've got a couple of other spots to make this afternoon."

"*We've* got a couple of other spots to make," Muggsy corrected him.

He started to argue, decided it was a lost cause, shrugged. "Okay, so *we've* got a couple of spots to make. That means we'd better get going."

CHAPTER SEVEN

THE HOUSE was an old, dilapidated tenement in a row of shabby buildings of similar vintage just off Houston Street in the shadow of the old el. Johnny Liddell led Muggsy Kiely into the dim vestibule, down the corridor to the door at the far end. He knocked, heard the sound of a panel sliding in the door.

The voice was old, raspy, smelled of stale beer, "Yeah?"

"It's Liddell. I want to see the Dummy."

The panel scraped shut, and after a moment the door creaked open. The room beyond was in darkness, but as soon as the door swung shut behind them a dim light went on.

The doorman was a thin, shriveled man in a collarless shirt. When he grinned, his toothless gums gleamed pink in the light. "Dummy's kind of tied up, Liddell," he said, "but he says come up and wait."

Liddell nodded. "You know Muggsy Kiely? Jim Kiely's kid."

The old man leered. "Knowed her ever since she was a kid, when her old man used to be a police reporter on the downtown beat." He nodded toward the stairs in the rear. "You better be getting up. The Dummy don't like to be kept waiting."

Liddell led the way up a flight of iron stairs in the rear of the apartment, came out in a huge room. The windows had been boarded over; there was no trace of the original partitions that separated the rooms. Along the walls, a group of dejected, bearded men lay sprawled, in varying positions. They stared incuriously at the newcomers.

"Dummy's office is up at the other end," Liddell explained.

They walked the length of the room, entered an unpainted wooden door. Inside there were a couple of rickety-looking chairs, a large desk with an oversized chair behind it. There was no one in the room.

"Dummy must be putting some of his new students through the paces," Liddell muttered. "Ever see the routine, Muggs?"

The girl shook her head. "Heard about it, but I've never seen it."

Liddell walked over to the far wall, felt around the molding until he located a cleverly hidden switch. He pressed it, stood aside while a camouflaged panel slid open. He stuck his head through, then withdrew it, motioned for Muggsy to join him.

Below, the entire floor of the house had been converted into a large auditorium. A group of ragged men, similar to the group waiting in the outer room, each with a sign proclaiming: *Blind or Deaf and Dumb* around their neck, were practicing.

"So that's Dummy's school for beggars," Muggsy whispered. "How does it work?"

Liddell grinned. "He's training them so they won't be shown up as fakers and hurt the profession." He pointed to a group wearing the *Deaf and Dumb* signs. "See those dummies? He keeps them practicing until they can have a gun shot off behind them without flinching before he assigns them a beat."

Muggsy shook her head. "A school for beggars! What a way to make a living…"

Liddell slid the panel shut. "It's like anything else. Begging has to be organized. Dummy not only trains them, but maps out their beats so they won't be running all over each other." He dropped onto one of the rickety chairs, which creaked ominously under his weight. "That makes the Dummy a very handy guy to know sometimes."

"Why? Business so bad in the detective line you're figuring on making a bid for a beat?"

Liddell grunted. "That could be, too. But with all his boys covering the city like a blanket, Dummy has thousands of eyes all over town. After all, who pays any attention to a beggar—particularly a blind beggar?"

Muggsy found a cigarette in her purse, lit it. "That's why you were so sure you could get faster results than Herlehy's eighteen thousand trained men, eh?"

"Why not? The guy I'm after is most likely to be hanging out in dives and honky-tonks where no self-respecting policeman would be caught dead." He reached over, snagged Muggsy's cigarettes, dumped one out for himself, settled back to wait.

They hadn't long to wait. After a few minutes the panel slid open, and the Dummy minced in. He was almost unbelievably fat, the rolls under his chin wagging from side to side as he walked, a caricature of a smile pasted on his pouting, overripe lips. He made directly for the chair behind the desk, sank into it with a sigh.

"Mr. Liddell. Always glad to see you, sir. And Miss Kiely. How is your father these days? He doesn't ever come to see the Dummy, as he did in the old days." His voice was blubbery, almost as if it were choked by the fat on his neck.

"Jim doesn't get around the way he used to, Dummy," Muggsy told him. "He speaks of you often, though."

The Dummy nodded, disturbing the multiple chins. His pig-like eyes played leapfrog from Muggsy to Johnny Liddell and back. "I'd like to think you were paying the old Dummy a social call," he breathed heavily, "but I'm afraid those days are past. What can I do for you?"

"I need some help, Dummy. I want to locate a guy. Fast."

The fat man leaned back, laced pudgy fingers across his middle, regarded Liddell from behind the discolored pouches that buttressed his eyes. "These things are often expensive, my good friend." He licked at his pouty lips with the tip of his tongue. "Sometimes very expensive."

"Not this time," Liddell told him. "This time it's a personal matter. It comes out of my own pocket."

The fat man clucked sympathetically. "Tell me about it."

"Guy's name is Lunfaro. He hires his gun out."

Dummy pursed his lips, dropped heavy, purple-veined lids over the small pig-like eyes. "Lunfaro's a bad boy, Liddell." He opened the small eyes, peered at his visitors. "That would cost at least five hundred."

Liddell snorted. "I'll give you a century."

The fat man's eyes looked hurt. "A hundred? That would hardly pay my overhead." He licked at his lips again. "Let's say two hundred. After all, I do have my expenses."

Liddell nodded. "Okay. Two hundred." He reached into his pocket, pulled out his wallet, laid the two fifties Hong had paid him on the desk. "A hundred now, a hundred after I get to talk to this guy."

The fat man, made an effort to hide his eagerness, tapped his stubby fingers on the edge of the desk, managed to keep his hands off the money. "I'll pass the word along immediately."

"How soon can I expect some action?"

"It depends, my good friend. Is the heat on our friend Lunfaro?"

Liddell shook his head. "There's no heat on him. He doesn't know I'm looking for him, and as of now the police don't want him."

The fat man nodded. "In that case it might even be tonight."

"It's got to be tonight if it's going to do me any good," Liddell told him. "I'm fighting time on this one."

The fat man pursed his lips, puffed out his cheeks. His eyes hadn't left the bills on the desk. Finally, he nodded, "Tonight."

"Good." Liddell got to his feet. "You have my office number and my home?"

The Dummy nodded, disturbing the rolls of fat under his chin.

"If I'm not home, call me at the office. I have an answering service. They'll take the message," Liddell told him.

The Dummy reached out for the bills, folded them lovingly, slid them into his jacket pocket. "You should be hearing from me within the next three or four hours." He leaned back; touched the tips of his fingers across his middle. "Lunfaro is a bad boy, Liddell. A very bad boy."

"Maybe I can persuade him to see the error of his ways." Liddell got up, helped Muggsy to her feet. "I'm counting on you, Dummy. Don't let me down."

The fat man nodded, wiped his thick lips with the back of his hand. "We'll do our best." He reached over, jabbed at the button on his desk with a pudgy forefinger.

"Yeah, Dummy?" the rasping voice of the guard at the front door came through a hidden speaker.

"Mr. Liddell and Miss Kiely are on their way out."

"Right." There was a click, and the connection went dead.

"I'll wait for your call, Dummy," Liddell told him. He led the way out of the office through the large outer room. The derelicts were still strewn along the wall, almost as though no one had moved since Liddell and Muggsy had last passed through.

Downstairs, the little man with the rasping voice and beery breath was waiting. "Didn't take you long. Must have been a cash job," he approved. "Never takes the Dummy long to make up his mind when the cash is on the line."

He opened the door for them, watched them through. "Tell your old man hello for me, Miss Kiely. Don't get to see him much any more."

The air in the street was a bracing relief after the closeness of the Dummy's "school." Liddell caught Muggsy's elbow, steered her toward the Bowery.

"Think Dummy can find Lunfaro, Johnny?" the blonde asked.

Liddell grunted. "If anyone can, he can. His boys are all over town, know everybody. They'll turn him up."

"Where are we going now?"

"You have a job, remember? I'm going to find you a cab and send you to work. One of us must have something coming in."

Muggsy consulted the tiny baguette on her wrist. "It's early," she protested. "It's hardly four and I'm not due until five-thirty."

Liddell shrugged. "Okay, baby. If you want to tag along, there are still a couple of social calls I've got to make."

"On whom?"

Liddell shrugged. "We've got a choice, looks like. There are three names we've dug up in this mess so far. Lunfaro, Hunt Brin, and Ben Cerla. Dummy's handling Lunfaro, Brin probably lives uptown, and Cerla has a place in Chinatown—only a few blocks from here."

"Then it's Cerla?"

"Right. Let's go down and see what it's like in Chinese Heaven."

The Chinese Heaven was a big, gaudy, three-story building erected in the heart of Chinatown by an architect with a fixation on the subject of pagodas. Its front was lavishly smeared with gilt and garish gingerbread; a hidden amplifier spilled tinny music into the street. A huge sign announced: *Chinese and American Menu. All legal beverages.*

Johnny Liddell and Muggsy Kiely shouldered their way along the narrow winding street toward the ornate, brightly colored canopy that proclaimed: *Chinese Heaven.* A doorman, dressed in loose-fitting Chinese robes that failed to disguise the shoulders of a professional bouncer, stood guard at the door. He twisted a battered face into a reasonable facsimile of a smile as he pushed the door open for them.

A red-carpeted, dimly lit hallway led to a long, brightly lighted modern bar. At the far end a couple was huddling over what appeared to be one of a series of Martinis, while a slightly faded blonde sat forlornly toying with a half-empty glass. She looked up hopefully as Liddell and Muggsy entered, the interest draining from her face when she saw the girl. She went back to making concentric circles on the bar with the wet bottom of her glass while Liddell piloted Muggsy to a pair of empty barstools.

The Chinese bartender sidled up, swabbed the bar with a damp cloth, waited.

"Harper and water for me. Seven Crown and ginger for the lady," Liddell told him.

While the bartender was selecting the bottles from the backbar, Liddell looked around. The bar ran what was apparently the width of the building. At the far end, a small passageway ran to the door marked Private. To the left, a large staircase led up to what were apparently the public dining rooms on the second and third floors.

The bartender slid two shot glasses in front of them, spilled the liquor in well above the mark on the glass. He added two setups, picked up a dollar bill and a quarter from the money Liddell dropped on the bar, shuffled off to the other end of the bar.

"Not a bad setup," Liddell commented. "Wonder if that's where friend Cerla hangs his hat." He nodded toward the door marked *Private*.

"You sure it's a good idea to go barging in on him like this, Johnny? Maybe we ought to leave him to Herlehy."

Liddell sipped at the bourbon, approved of the effect, tossed it off. "What could Herlehy do? He can't pick him up and question him. On what charge? Me, I don't need a charge." He slid off the barstool. "All I have to do is drop in and have a talk."

"Be careful, Johnny. Cerla is bad medicine."

Liddell nodded, ambled to the end of the bar, headed for the door marked *Private*. A small, dapper Chinese with damp, reproachful eyes materialized at his side.

"You're going in the wrong direction, mister," he told Liddell. His right hand was sunk wrist-deep in his jacket pocket. "It's on the other side. It says 'Men' on the door." He stood in front of Liddell, blocking his way.

"Ben Cerla wants to see me," Liddell told him.

The Chinese's eyes never left Liddell's face. The right hand stayed in the jacket pocket. With his left hand he fumbled in his breast pocket, brought out a typewritten flimsy. His dark, liquid eyes dropped to the list. "What name?"

"Liddell. Johnny Liddell."

The damp eyes rolled upward from the paper. The face was even more reproachful. "Very funny, mister." He stepped closer until Liddell could feel the muzzle of the gun in his side. "Ben Cerla doesn't want to see you. If I were you, I'd go away. Fast."

"Cerla wants to see me, all right. Maybe he doesn't know it yet but he wants to see me bad," Liddell grunted. "Tell him I'm out here. Tell him I'm an old friend of his. And Hong's. And Lunfaro's. We're all buddies."

The Chinese stared fixedly at him. Then, without any change of expression, he turned his back, walked to the door marked *Private* knocked three times. It clicked open, swallowed up his thin-shouldered figure. After a moment he was back, the same reproachful look in his eyes, the hand back in his pocket. But now the hand in the pocket seemed to be pointing at a spot roughly an inch below Liddell's umbilicus.

"You must be psychic. He does want to see you."

"I'll read your tea leaves some day if you're a good boy," Liddell promised.

"Do that. Or better still, I'll check you with my Ouija board." He stepped aside, motioned Liddell in.

The room beyond was a sharp contrast to the garishness and pseudo-Chinese *decor* of the rest of the building. It was small, comfortable. A gray-green carpet covered the floor from wall to wall, giving it a subdued, soothing quality. A number of easy chairs were set around the room, and in the corner, behind a large executive desk, a man sat playing solitaire.

He looked up as Liddell came in, squinted at him nearsightedly. He was out of place in the restfulness of the surroundings. His thin, pinched face was heavily pockmarked, his left eye twitched endlessly as he studied the private detective. He sat in his shirtsleeves, shoulder holster in place, the heavy butt of a .45 sticking out. An immaculate pearl-gray fedora was perched on the back of his head.

"He heeled, Sing?" he wanted to know.

The guard stepped up behind Liddell, jabbed the snout of his gun in his back, fanned him expertly. He slid the .45 out of its holster, pushed it across the desk to Cerla.

Liddell grinned humorlessly. "That's twice in twenty-four hours somebody has taken that gun away from me. The next time I pass it over, it'll be one slug at a time."

"You'll scare us to death," Cerla snorted. He picked up the .45, examined it, laid it on the corner of the desk. "Wait outside, Sing. This won't take long." He waited until the door had closed behind the small Chinese.

"Okay, wise guy. What's on your mind? What's the idea of busting in here like this?"

"I wanted to ask you a couple of questions."

The left eye twitched maddeningly. "About what?"

"Murder. A client of mine named Hong. I understood he was an associate of yours."

Cerla picked a ragged cigar butt from the ashtray at his elbow, jammed it between his teeth. "What do you mean, client? You a peeper?"

Liddell nodded. "That's right."

Cerla's thin lip twisted up in a sneer. "Go on back to peeping through keyholes. Blow."

Liddell felt through his pockets for cigarettes, found none, walked over to the desk, helped himself to a pack on the desk. "Like I said, Hong was a client of mine before he was killed. He said if anything happened to him to get in touch with you."

"You're a liar. I never heard of him." The man behind the desk got up from his chair, walked around the desk, stood in front of Liddell, tapped him on the chest. "I don't like peepers in general. I don't like you in particular. Get in my way and I'll stamp you flat. Now act smart like you think you are and get out of here and stay out." His thin lips twisted into what could have passed for a smile. "A guy like you could get awful unlucky awful fast, and I wouldn't want it to happen in my joint."

Liddell shrugged. "Well, if that's the way you feel about it, I guess I might just as well turn Hong's package over to the cops."

A wary look came into Cerla's eyes. He pulled the butt from his mouth, examined the soggy end, pasted back a loose leaf with the tip of his tongue. "What package?"

"The package your boys have been ripping my office to ribbons trying to find."

Cerla's eyes narrowed to thin slits. He jammed the cigar back between his teeth, walked back to the desk, jabbed a button. There was a buzz at the door, and the Chinese guard walked in. He stood behind Liddell.

"This guy's a peeper. Take care of him, Sing," he growled.

The Chinese pulled his hand from his pocket. An ugly snub-nosed .38 was clenched in his fist. "You wanted to see Cerla so bad, mister. Now you've seen him. Let's you and me take a walk."

Liddell grinned bleakly. "I forgot to mention that I left a friend out at the bar, and I did happen to mention to Inspector Herlehy down at headquarters that I was dropping by here."

Cerla glared at him, the bad eye twitching endlessly. He swore under his breath. "Get him out of here Sing. Make sure nothing happens to him while he's still on the premises."

The guard caught Liddell by the arm, swung him around. Liddell chopped down at the guard's wrist, hit him in the face with an open hand that slammed him back against the wall. The Chinese slid to a sitting position on the floor, raised the .38.

"Put up the rod, Sing," Cerla barked. "I told you no rough stuff while he's in here."

The Chinese's hand shook, his knuckles white around the gun. He got himself under control with an effort, pulled himself to his feet. "I'll be seeing you, Liddell," he promised.

"Sure you will. Every time you turn around." Liddell deliberately turned his back on the guard, held his hand out. "My gun."

"Yeah. You may need it," Cerla told him. He handed the gun across the desk, watched while Liddell fitted it back into its holster. He turned, walked past the guard, slammed the door behind him.

At the bar, Muggsy greeted him nervously. "What's been keeping you? I saw that little gunsel go back in there. I thought sure you were in trouble. What've you been doing?"

"Just lighting a fire under Cerla. I as much as told him I still had the package."

"You what?" Muggsy groaned. "Why?"

Liddell shrugged. "Just to get things moving." He signaled to the bartender, who was just returning a telephone to its cradle, indicated refills.

The bartender nodded, caught two bottles from the backbar on the way down. He set the bottles on the bar, scooped up the setup glasses, washed them behind the bar, dumped fresh ice and water in Liddell's, slid it across the bar to him. Then he filled the two shot glasses from the bottles, turned to replace them on the backbar.

Liddell brought out a roll of bills, separated a ten from the rest, folded it so the man behind the bar could see the denomination. "What's your name, bud?" he asked the man behind the stick.

"Soong," the bartender told him, his eyes fixed on the bill.

"Like to earn this?" Liddell held out the ten-spot.

The bartender looked up and down the bar, nodded, "Sure."

"Okay. I'll drink the bourbon. You drink the water, and it's yours."

The vitality oozed out of the broad grin on the bartender's face, leaving it a hollow mask. His dark eyes looked trapped. "I don't know what you mean."

Liddell pushed the setup glass across the bar. "It's only water. *Drink it.*"

The Chinese's eyes flicked right and left. He shook his head. "I can't. House rules. I'd lose my job." He started to draw away.

Liddell reached across the bar, caught a handful of the barman's jacket, yanked him forward until he was bent across the bar, his face a few inches from Liddell's. "I ought to pour it down your throat."

Perspiration beaded the barman's face. He shook his head vigorously, tried to squirm away.

Liddell shoved him back violently, almost upsetting the backbar. "Tell Cerla he's losing his touch. I'm allergic to poisoned ice cubes." He turned his back on the bartender, helped Muggsy off her stool.

"A Mickey?" she asked.

Liddell nodded. "Cerla doesn't waste any time. I told you I set a fire under him. I didn't expect it to get so hot so fast."

CHAPTER EIGHT

JOHNNY LIDDELL personally delivered Muggsy Kiely to the front door of the *Advance* office. Then, passing up the string of taxis out front, he headed back across town on foot. He was so lost in speculation that he failed to notice the big black sedan that swung in to the curb at his side until a harsh voice behind him said, "There's somebody wants to have a talk with you, Liddell."

The man was big-framed, hard-eyed. He kept his hand sunk deep into his jacket pocket as he talked. Behind him stood a second man, a third sat at the wheel of the big car.

"Is it formal or should I come as I am?" Liddell grunted.

The hard-eyed man motioned toward the open door of the car, stepped aside to let Liddell pass him. Liddell shrugged, walked over to the car. The second man took his position on Liddell's far side, effectively flanking him.

For a moment, Liddell debated the advisability of resisting, decided it was suicide, got into the car. The two men followed, took positions on either side of him.

As soon as the car door had slammed shut behind them, the motor roared into life and the big car hurtled forward. It bore right, past the unsightly pile of bricks that constituted Knickerbocker Village, shot up the East Side Drive.

At the 60th Street exit, the driver expertly separated it from the stream of uptown-bound cars, pulled off the Drive, and headed for the lower level of the Queensboro Bridge. Once across the bridge, the car melted into the line headed east on Long Island, swung onto Northern Boulevard.

"What's this all about?" Liddell asked the hard-eyed man.

The man shrugged, pulled a pack of cigarettes from his pocket, held it to Liddell. "You'll find out when we get there," he told him.

Liddell accepted a cigarette, lit it, settled back to watch the character of the neighborhood change from densely populated to suburban, with bigger and bigger stretches of unpopulated areas showing up. About forty minutes out from the bridge, they passed the outside limit of New York City, headed into Nassau County.

"In the old days, they used to do the job in New Jersey," Liddell grunted. "Times change."

The hard-eyed man offered no comment, leaned forward, whispered into the driver's ear.

The car skidded to a stop at the side of the road. Liddell looked around. They were parked right on Northern Boulevard, outside a brightly-lighted garage. Across the street a sputtering neon proclaimed: *115 Club*.

"This is as far as we go," the hard-eyed man told Liddell. He waited while the driver got out, opened the car door on his side. "He'll take you where you're to go."

Liddell scowled his bewilderment, followed instructions. The driver led the way across the heavily traveled highway, into the 115 Club. Inside, a smiling little man who bore an amazing resemblance to Frank McHugh of the movies stepped up to them.

"Where's Mr. Byers sitting, Frank?" the driver asked.

The little man led the way to a booth in the dining room right off the bar.

There were three men sitting at the table in the booth. One of them was the man who had come to his office with Treasury Department credentials and had taken the package with him. Liddell looked around, saw the place was filled with people. He estimated his chances of making a break, concluded they were good, decided to stay to see what was going to happen.

"So you're Liddell?" The speaker was an elderly man, thick white hair framing a full, ruddy face. "My name is Byers. Treasury Department."

Liddell grinned mirthlessly. "You, too?"

"I don't blame you for being confused, Liddell," the white-haired man grinned. "When you called my office yesterday to check on our friend here," he nodded toward the man at his table, "I had no choice but to lie to you. It happens that our friend is a government man, but his name happens to be Gerken, not Byers. He used my credentials because he does not happen to be connected with Treasury. That clear?"

"Clear as mud," Liddell complained. His eyes hopscotched from face to face at the table. "How do I know this is on the level?"

"Perhaps you'll take my word for the fact that this gentlemen is Byers," the third man at the table interposed. He tossed an impressive array of credentials on the table in front of Liddell. "My name is Graham. Larry Graham. I'm one of the United States representatives at the United Nations Council here at Lake Success."

Liddell flipped through the credentials, seemed satisfied, passed them back to Graham. "Why all the secrecy?" He nodded toward Gerken. "If he'd told me he was fed, I would have turned the package over to him without all this cloak-and-dagger routine."

Graham stuffed the credentials back into his pocket. "Sit down and have a drink. Maybe we can give you enough insight into what this is all about to answer all your questions."

Liddell slid into the booth, told the waiter he'd settle for bourbon and water, waited.

"Suppose you tell him, Byers," Graham suggested.

The Treasury man nodded. "Okay. You two can fill in if I skip anything important." He leaned back in the booth, studied Liddell's face for a moment as if trying to decide where to begin. "I suppose you want to know about the package?"

Liddell nodded.

"We expected that package to be very important to us, Liddell." He indicated Gerken with a toss of his head. "As I just told you, our friend Gerken, here, is a government man, but not with Treasury." He looked around casually, dropped his voice. "He's assigned to counterespionage. Hong, too, was a counterespionage agent."

Liddell looked closely to see whether or not the man was serious. "Hong?"

Byers nodded. "He was working on a very important mission. We were hoping that package would contain some vital information." He shook his head. "It didn't. At least, not enough."

Liddell waited until the waiter had placed a glass and a shot of bourbon in front of him. "But why leave it with me?"

"He had no choice," Byers explained. "The people he was watching had gotten suspicious. He was afraid he was being tailed, and knew it would be fatal to try to contact us at headquarters. Your name was familiar to him because of some work you had done on the Coast. He left it there, called us immediately to pick it up."

"Why didn't Gerken tell me this when he picked up the package?"

"He couldn't. In the first place, it might endanger Hong's life. At that time we didn't know he was marked for death. In the second place, officially as a federal agency, we wouldn't want to have it known that we're on the case."

Liddell nodded, mixed his drink, tasted it.

Byers grinned at him. "I don't mind telling you you gave us a bad moment when you remembered Judge Mason as the signer of the writ, but the judge managed to carry it off very well."

"Why are you telling me this now?"

Byers looked from Liddell to the U.N. representative. "Suppose you take it on from there, Graham."

Graham nodded. "We thought it only fair to bring you up to date on what's been happening. As you can imagine, this could easily be embarrassing to the State Department if it got undue publicity. We wanted you to know what was at stake before you got into it too deeply."

"What you're getting ready to say is that you'd rather I kept my nose out of this and let your own boys handle it?"

Graham smiled. "Not quite that bluntly. What I was driving at is that you need no longer feel that you must find Hong's killer because he was your client. We'll handle that for you. After all, the fee Hong paid you would hardly—"

"I have another client who wants the killer," Liddell interrupted.

The diplomatic attaché frowned. "Another client?" He turned to Byers. "You told me nothing about another client."

"I didn't know," the Treasury man confessed. "Could you tell us who he is without violating any confidences, Liddell?"

Liddell considered it, shrugged. "I don't see there's any secret about it. Jimmy Kaiming has commissioned the agency to find Hong's killer."

Byers pursed his lips, plucked at the lower one with his fingers. "Kaiming? From the tong?"

Liddell nodded.

"I didn't know he knew Hong," Gerken put in quietly.

"He didn't," Liddell told them. "Kaiming's only interest in the case is the fact that one of his countrymen was knocked off. He didn't want to work through the police, so he's hired me to handle it privately."

Byers drummed on the edge of the table with his fingertips. "That does make a difference," he admitted. He looked at the diplomatic attaché. "How about it, Graham?"

Graham stroked the side of his chin with his fingertips. "There's nothing we can do about it. Even if we did persuade Liddell to back out on his commitment, Kaiming might put another agency on the job, one we couldn't be as sure of." He stared at Liddell. "Maybe you'd better stay on the case."

"I intended to," Liddell told him.

"You know that you can look for no help from us?" Byers reminded him. "Although Hong was one of our boys, officially we can't even admit his existence."

Liddell grinned. "I'm not looking for help. But it might save me a lot of time if somebody were to whisper in my ear what was in that package that makes it so important."

The Treasury man and Graham both looked at Gerken. He nodded. "I think he has a right to know."

"You're the boss." Byers shrugged. He turned back to Liddell. "Hong was on the trail of an international gang of extortionists. Hot on their trail."

Liddell took a drink from his glass, put it down on the table. "What kind of extortionists?"

"Kidnapers," Byers told him. "They were shaking down well-to-do American Chinese for ransom for relatives who had fallen into the hands of a certain group of Chinese bandits in their native land." He pursed his lips, seemed to be selecting his words carefully. "His report was very incomplete and sketchy. It did not give us the information we need to crack down on the American contact of these bandits."

Liddell nodded. "But it did mention some names?"

"Most of it was guesswork," Gerken put in.

"Did it, for instance, mention a Ben Cerla or a Hunt Brin or a Dominick Lunfaro?" Liddell persisted.

The counterespionage man's eyes narrowed. "Why do you ask?"

"We won't get any place if we keep answering one question with another. Did Hong's report mention any of those three?"

Gerken looked to the diplomatic attaché for permission, got it. "Hunt Brin was mentioned. Ben Cerla was mentioned. There was no mention of the other man."

Liddell nodded. "What did he have to say about Brin and Cerla?"

"Just suspicions. As you may know, Brin has a background full of shady deals. You know him?"

Liddell shook his head. "Not yet."

"Well, he could fit into the picture. So could Cerla. But we still don't know where either of them fit, if at all." He drank from his glass, regarded Liddell over the rim. "We could pick a lot of the stooges up tomorrow, but that won't get us the big brains behind this operation. He's the one we want. Hong almost had him and was killed because of it."

"I understand. I've played for keeps before," Liddell grunted.

"You understand that everything we've told you here tonight is highly confidential, Liddell?" Graham, the diplomatic attaché, pointed out.

Liddell nodded.

"We won't interfere with you in your murder investigation, nor will we aid it in anyway. However, we must insist that you restrict your investigation to the murder aspect."

"All I want is the killer for my client," Liddell assured him. "I'll leave the cloak-and-dagger stuff to your boys."

Graham nodded, looked relieved. "I'm glad we understand each other." He drained his glass, set it back on the table. "We're going to have some dinner here, if you can stay and join us. I have a late Security Council meeting at Lake Success and I have to stay pretty close to base."

Liddell consulted his watch, shook his head. "I'm expecting a pretty important message at the office. I'll take a rain check on that dinner."

Graham nodded, extending his hand. "Good hunting."

The telephone jangled so hard on the corner of the desk it seemed as though it was about to jump off onto the floor. Johnny Liddell stirred in his desk chair, opened his eyes groggily, stared around at the wreckage of his office.

The new filing cabinets had been torn apart, their contents strewn all over the floor. The front of his new desk was scarred and split where somebody had ripped the lock out with a jimmy. The destruction spread to all items in the office.

The phone jangled again.

Liddell let his feet drop from the corner of the desk, hit the floor with a jar that made him swear under his breath. He reached out, snagged the phone from its cradle.

"Yeah?"

"This Liddell?" a wheezing voice demanded metallically.

"Yeah. Speaking."

There was a slight pause. "You was talking to a friend today about some guy you was wanting to meet up with. Remember the friend's name?"

"The Dummy."

The receiver sounded satisfied. "This guy you was wanting to meet. There's a party at the Hotel Breen. He just breezed in."

"The Breen? On Forty-seventh?"

The voice nodded. "That's the joint. Party's strictly private. A tea party for a lot of society jerks on the make for a thrill."

"How do I get in?"

"Signal's 'Louis.' It'll cost you a sawbuck at the door. Going to get rough?"

"Why?"

The receiver cackled with a shrill laugh. "It ain't because I'm afraid any of my friends is going to get hurt, that's for sure."

Liddell nodded impatiently. "So what's the difference if it gets rough?"

"I just thought you might like to know that if you decide to leave in a hurry, the door marked 'Service' takes you out into an alley connecting with Forty-eighth Street."

"Thanks. I'll remember that."

The receiver cackled again, then clicked as the connection was broken.

Liddell dropped his receiver back on the hook, took another look around his office, swore fervently. He checked his .45, dropped an extra clip into his jacket pocket, clipped the gun into his shoulder holster. At the corner sink, he dashed water on his face, scrubbed it dry with a towel. Then, letting himself out of his office, he headed for the night elevator bank.

CHAPTER NINE

THE BREEN WAS an old weather-beaten stone building nestled in a row of similarly weather-beaten buildings that line the north side of 47th Street between Broadway and Sixth Avenue. A small plaque to the right of the door dispelled any lingering doubts as to its character by announcing it as the Hotel Breen.

A threadbare and faded carpet ran the length of a lobby that had long since given up any pretense of serving any useful purpose. The chairs were rickety and unsafe, the artificial rubber plants grimed with dust.

Johnny Liddell ignored the old man behind the registration desk who raised watery eyes as Liddell passed, then dropped them back to a perusal of the scratch sheet spread out on the desk. Liddell made directly for the lone elevator cage in the rear. A pimpled youth with slack mouth and discolored sacs under his eyes stared dully at him as he approached.

"Louis's place," Liddell told him. "What floor's it on?"

The slack mouth twisted into a wet smear of a grin, the operator winked one eye obscenely, slammed the elevator door shut. "Sixth. That joint must really be jumping tonight." He watched the floors crawl by the open grillwork of the door. "Wish I could sneak off for a few minutes and smoke me a stick."

The elevator jerked to a spine-jarring stop, the operator slammed back the grilled door. "It's six-o-eight." He indicated a door at the far end of the hall, stood in his cage, watched Liddell until he had reached the door.

A narrow-chested man with thick, wavy hair opened the door in response to Liddell's knock. He looked Liddell over carelessly. "Looks like you're in the wrong room, mister. This is a private party."

"That's funny. Louis told me to drop by," Liddell told him. He held out his hand, a ten-spot between his fingers.

"Friend of Louis's, eh? That's different." The narrow chested man brought his right hand out of his pocket, clamped it damply around Liddell's. When it was with-drawn, the bill had gone with it. "Come on in." He stepped out of the doorway, waited until Liddell was in the outer room, closed the door behind him. From another closed door, Liddell caught light snatches of laughter and the sounds of a party in full, hilarious progress.

"Sounds like it's beginning to jump," Liddell commented.

"It'll get better," Narrow Chest assured him. He bolted the hall door, led the way across the room. He opened the other door, pushed aside the heavy curtain that was hung from ceiling to floor as a means of deadening the noise.

Inside, a radio-phonograph combination was grinding out a frenzied rhythm beat, while half a dozen or more couples danced sensuously on the floor. The chairs and the sofa had been pushed back against the wall to give the dancers more room. Thick, oily smoke swirled lazily around the one indirect light in the room, filling the air with a sickish-sweet aroma.

Liddell looked around the room, failed to see Lunfaro, the hood whose picture Muggsy had picked out at police headquarters as the gunman who had worked him over at Luigi's. He ambled through the man-made fog toward an open door that apparently led to the adjoining room. As he approached the door he could hear the low mutter of conversation spiced by the rattle of dice, the click of a roulette wheel.

He wandered in. A group of men and women stood huddled around a portable roulette setup in one corner, while against the other wall a half-dozen men were following the progress of a hot crap game. Liddell's eyes roved over each of the men in turn, saw none that looked like the picture at headquarters.

In the background of the crowd, a tall blond man in a double-breasted tuxedo looked disturbingly familiar. Liddell tried to place him, finally narrowed him down to an old news clipping that Muggsy Kiely had shown him. The man in the tuxedo was Hunt Brin.

There was a groan of dismay from the direction of the crap game as the shooter crapped out. Two men got up disgustedly, brushed off their knees. Liddell recognized one of them as Ben Cerla. He made an attempt to back out of the door, stopped when he realized Cerla had recognized him.

Liddell could read the shock of recognition in the racketeer's eyes. Cerla looked for a moment as though he was going to make for Liddell thought better of it, signaled for Hunt Brin.

The blond man frowned his displeasure at the summons, shouldered his way through the players, listened impatiently while Cerla whispered in his ear. After a moment, Brin looked up, his eyes rested negligently on Liddell. He nodded briefly, shook off Cerla's restraining hand, gave an almost imperceptible signal to the two tuxedoed guards who were trying, with no success, to look inconspicuous.

Hunt Brin walked over to where Liddell stood in the doorway. "I'm afraid we haven't had the pleasure of meeting you." His smile was pleasant, lazy. His eyes were cold blue chips. He reached up, fiddled with the tips of the white handkerchief in his breast pocket. "I'm afraid these are rather exclusive gatherings and we cannot permit sightseers." He lowered his voice confidentially. "You can understand that when my friends let their hair down and relax, they don't like a lot of strangers around."

"A couple of puffs of that stuff they're smoking back there and they wouldn't know Polly Adler from their own mother." Liddell grinned back.

"Everyone to his own taste, Liddell." The lazy smile was still there, the eyes cold, hard. "Some people like to kill themselves that way, others go out asking for it other ways."

Liddell nodded. "So I hear. Anyway, I'm not exactly a stranger. I'm a friend of Louis."

"How interesting. You see, I'm Louis. And I've never seen you before in my life." The two tuxedoed guards had somehow joined them in the doorway. "I think probably there's been some mistake, Liddell. I hope you'll be cooperative and that there'll be no trouble."

Liddell looked at the two guards, back to Brin, shrugged. "Why should there be any trouble? I just heard there might be some fun in here tonight and wandered in."

"Of course." Brin smiled coldly. "I know that if you had known it was a private party you never would have crashed it." His eyes flowed from Liddell to the tuxedoed man at his right. "See that Liddell has a drink before he goes, Tim."

Liddell's eyes scanned the faces of the people in the room. There was still no sign of the hood, Lunfaro. "As a matter of fact, I was just leaving. I thought I might see a friend of mine in here and I wanted to have a word with him." He looked around again. "I don't see him around, though."

Hunt Brin rearranged the points of his pocket-handkerchief, flicked at an imaginary piece of lint on the midnight blue of his tuxedo. "Anybody I know?"

"You might. His name's Lunfaro. He doesn't care who he rents his gun out to."

"Sounds fascinating," Brin drawled. The cold blue chips of his eyes regarded Liddell from behind their lids. "I've never heard of him. Maybe the boys know him. Ever hear of a Lunfaro, Tim?"

Neither man changed expression. Neither moved his eyes from Liddell's face. Both shook their heads.

"You see, Liddell?" Brin smiled. "We've never heard of your friend." He nodded to the two guards. "I think Mr. Liddell is ready to leave now, Tim."

The two guards closed in on Liddell, flanked him as he walked back through the room where the phonograph ground out the be-bop endlessly. The dancers had evidently given up the effort, were sprawled on the couches and on each others' laps in the chairs that lined the room.

A tall, deep-chested woman, her brassy blond hair piled high on her head in a stylish coiffure, was serving murky-looking drinks from a silver tray. Johnny Liddell decided that she looked better than she had the last time he saw her—in the sleazy flat downstairs from the apartment where a skinny little Chinese named Hong had screamed away his life less than twenty-four hours ago. He had little time to wonder what a Chinatown hustler named Goldy LaTour was doing at a café-society brawl before the two uniformed guards had ushered him to, and through, the doorway into the hall.

Back on 47th Street, Johnny Liddell headed west to Broadway. He stopped near the corner, stared glumly down the brightly lighted thoroughfare. A tall blonde with a fur piece hung carelessly around her neck stopped to look in Liggett's window, caught Liddell's eye in the reflection, cocked an eyebrow speculatively. Liddell returned the speculation with a frank appraisal, was interrupted by a tug on his sleeve.

"Need some shoelaces or razor blades, mister?" a high-pitched voice whined at his elbow.

Liddell dipped his free hand into his jacket pocket, came up with a hand full of change, dumped it into the man's outstretched hand. "Have a drink on me, pop."

"Thanks, mister," the voice whined. Then, with no visible movement of his lips. "Lunfaro ducked just before you got there."

Liddell started, realized the man was one of the Dummy's "eyes." He ran the back of his hand across his lips. "Get a line on where he went?"

"Try Kennedy's. Lunfaro has a babe in the floorshow. Her name's Nancy. Nancy Ryan." His eyelids dropped over his eyes like heavily veined film. He touched the greasy brim of his hat with a gnarled finger. "Thanks, mister," the whining voice piped up. He shuffled off, got lost in the fast-moving crowd.

Johnny Liddell elbowed himself a niche in the bar in Kennedy's. It was a smoky subcellar with thick clouds of smoke making visibility something less than zero. He ordered a shot of bourbon, waited until the bartender had slid it in front of him, passed a bill across the bar. The bartender started for the cash register. Liddell called him back. "Never mind the change, bud."

The bartender stopped, examined the bill. "You got us mixed up with the Stork, mister. We don't get a fin a shot here."

Liddell dumped his bourbon into the water, tasted it, approved. "Thought you might like to do me a favor."

"Depends."

Liddell's eyes flicked to the left, then right, leaned across the bar confidentially. "I was thinking of making a play for one of the babes in the show. Thought you might like to give me the proper knockdown."

"That wouldn't be no favor," the bartender grunted. He peered past Liddell to the floor where a group of girls were making a heroic, though losing, effort to keep time with the orchestra. "Well, every man to his taste. Which one?"

"Nancy."

The bartender scowled. "Ryan?"

Liddell nodded.

"Nancy's got a guy, mister. A guy who don't like competition." He looked around, dropped his voice. "A gun."

Liddell shrugged. "He's not worrying me. How about it?"

The bartender stared at him, sucked contemplatively on a back tooth, shrugged. "It's your skin. If you like holes in it, that's your business." He squinted into the glare of the floor lights. "Her number comes on next. You can at least get a look at what you're bidding on, in case you want to change your mind."

"Fair enough." Liddell nodded.

The bartender folded the five, dropped it into his watch pocket, walked down to the other end of the bar. On the floor, the band struggled with a fanfare, the lights went down, and a spotlight picked out the wasp-waisted, slightly effeminate figure of the master of ceremonies as he fluttered across the floor to the microphone. He told a few off-color jokes, sang two choruses of an old song nasally, then held up his hands to cut off the nonexistent applause.

"At this time we take pleasure in bringing out for your approval the star of our show—Miss Nancy Ryan," he barked into the mike.

The spot left him abruptly, shot to the far side of the bandstand, picking out a rhinestoned curtain. The curtain parted, and a tall, full-breasted brunette came out onto the floor. She wore a dark-red, strapless evening gown as though she had been poured into it. As she crossed the floor to the microphone, her every movement was suggestive, sensuous. She seemed to flow as though her body were completely boneless.

Her voice, when she started to sing, was low, throaty. The lyrics of her song were blue and off color, but her face maintained an expression of untroubled innocence. At the end of her number, she bowed to the burst of applause, paid no noticeable attention to the wolf calls and whistles, permitted herself to be coaxed into another, bluer number. This time she refused to give an encore, undulated back toward the dressing-room door.

Liddell turned back, grinned at the bartender's questioning stare. "How about it? Do I get the knockdown?"

The man behind the stick shrugged. "It's your funeral mister." He shuffled up to the service end of the bar where a waiter was unloading a tray of empty glasses, whispered to him. The waiter looked down to where Liddell was standing, shook his head. The bartender fished in his watch pocket, brought out the folded bill, let the waiter look at it. The waiter nodded, abandoned his tray of empties, walked down to where Liddell stood.

"Harry says you want I should deliver a message backstage." He snuffled. "I don't know, Kennedy don't like that kind of stuff."

Liddell nodded, found a folded five in his palm, stared at it significantly. "That's too bad. But I guess a rule's a rule, eh?"

The waiter reached out, snagged the folded bill, smoothed it out lovingly, transferred it to his vest pocket. A smile disarranged his battered features. "Sure, but it's like they say. A customer's got some rights. Who'll I say wants to see her?"

Liddell winked. "Just tell her it's a lonesome out-of-towner."

"Check." The waiter squinted into the smoke, located an empty table. "See the table near the post? You sit there, I'll bring her out. She ain't allowed to sit at the bar."

Liddell nodded, finished his drink, winked at the bartender. He picked his way through the crowded tables to the empty one the waiter had indicated. After a few minutes the waiter was back. "She'll be right with you, mister."

Liddell was on his third drink when he saw the tall brunette come out of the backstage door. She had changed the red evening gown for a low-cut black dress that provided an equally breathtaking showcase for her obvious assets. She stood at the bandstand, staring around with a frown until the waiter with the battered face caught her eye. He signaled her over, indicated Liddell. The frown faded from her face and she started toward him, picking her way between the tables.

Liddell stood up as she reached his table. "Thanks for coming out."

The brunette pursed thick, soft-looking lips, looked with approval at the broad shoulders, the thick shock of dark hair shot with gray. "I didn't know there were any out-of-towners looked like you," she said huskily. "They're usually fat, old, and drooling." She was older than she had looked on the floor. A faint network of wrinkles under her eyes was waging a losing battle with her make-up. There was a tired droop at the corners of the full lips.

"I'm not very old or fat." Liddell grinned.

The brunette's answering grin was quick, erased years from her face. She dropped into her chair, watched Liddell from under beaded eyelashes. "What made you ask me to come out?"

Liddell signaled for two drinks. "You kidding?"

The brunette pursed her lips, purred. "There are other pretty girls in the show. Why me? Why not one of them?"

"Maybe you're my type." Liddell held out a pack of cigarettes, waited until she had selected one, then took one himself, hung it from the corner of his mouth. "I hope you didn't mind my asking you to come out?"

Nancy leaned over, accepted a light, blew a stream of smoke up into his face. "I'm glad you did." She leaned back in her chair, studied him through dreamy, half-closed eyes. "Going to be around long?"

"If you want me to be."

A thin stream of smoke dribbled from between the girl's full lips. "What's really on your mind?"

"I don't follow."

"You're no out-of-towner. You've got the Big Town stamped all over you. And you're no sucker. You're not sitting here in this clip joint buying me cold tea at a buck and a half a throw just for excitement." She shrugged. "Not that I care, but why?"

Liddell twirled his butt between thumb and forefinger, stared at it. He decided to play it straight. "Maybe I wanted to meet you because I thought you and I could do some business together."

The brunette's eyes moved languidly from Liddell to the bar in the outer room, then from table to table. "What kind of business?"

"I'm in the market for information. I'm willing to pay for it."

"What makes you think I have the information you want?"

Liddell picked up his glass, swirled the liquor around the inside. "I know you have." He held the glass to his lips, studied her over the rim. "What do you say?"

"This is no place to talk," the brunette told him. She took a deep drag on her cigarette, held it out, stared at the crimson-stained end with distaste. "I've got a boyfriend who's crazy jealous. He might get the wrong idea."

Liddell nodded. "Where?"

The girl looked up. "My place?" She crushed out her cigarette in the ashtray on the table. "We don't have to worry about one of Dom's stooges playing chaperon."

"Suits me. Where and when? Want me to pick you up?"

"No. Meet me at my place." Her eyes swept the faces of the others in the place, her lips barely moved. "Carteret Apartments. Two D. I get finished here about three-thirty. Make it any time after four."

CHAPTER TEN

THE CARTERET APARTMENTS turned out to be a high stooped old brownstone on the West Side at 68th Street. It was one of a whole block of identical brownstones, most of which offered furnished rooms "with or without board." The Carteret, however, boasted a gold leaf lettered legend on the glass pane of its front door proclaiming: *Carteret Apartments—Accommodations for the Discriminating.*

Liddell climbed the high stone stoop, tried the vestibule door. It was open. On the hall door there was a cardboard sign that urged *Please Be Sure This Door Is Closed After You.* Whoever had used it last apparently didn't believe in signs.

Liddell pushed the door open, made sure it was closed behind him. There was no elevator; a flight of uncarpeted stairs led to the upper stories.

Apartment 2D was second floor front. Liddell knocked softly, waited for some indication from within. After a moment, he repeated his knock. There was no answer.

He tried the doorknob, found it locked. He debated the wisdom of breaking in, lost the decision, brought out a handful of keys. The third one he tried opened the door. He stepped in, closed the door behind him. The room was in darkness. He stood still, waited until his eyes had accustomed themselves to the darkness. There was no sound from anywhere in the apartment.

Liddell slid his .45 from its holster, reached for the light switch. Two table lamps bathed the room with a subdued light. There was nobody in the room. Liddell investigated the other two rooms, found them empty. He returned the .45 to its hammock, dropped into an easy chair to wait. His watch said 4:20.

It was nearly five when he heard a key being fitted into the lock. The door swung open, and the brunette stood in the doorway. Behind her stood Lunfaro!

Liddell's hand streaked for his .45, lost the race. Lunfaro covered him with a .38 that looked the size of a cannon. He pushed the girl in in front of him, closed the door.

"What kind of a double cross is this?" he growled. The color had drained from the girl's face, leaving her make-up as blotchy patches against the pallor. "It—it's no double cross, Dom," her husky voice quavered. "He's just a guy—a guy I met at the place. He's just—"

The gunman lashed out with his free hand, caught her across the face. "He's just a private eye, that's all. A guy that's been trying to put the finger on me all over town."

The girl rubbed the tips of her fingers over the angry red stain his slap had caused. "I'm sorry, mister," she told Liddell. "When he showed up I kept hanging around, hoping you'd get tired of waiting and go away."

Lunfaro reached out, slapped her again. "You'll be sorrier when I get through with you." He shoved her toward the bedroom door. "We'll talk it over when I get through with this peeper."

The girl started to protest, decided against it, put the back of her hand against the welt on her face. She walked to the bedroom door, closed it after her.

The gunman walked over to Liddell, motioned him to his feet. He relieved him of his .45, tossed it on the table. "You've been looking all over town for me. So now you've found me, peeper. What's on your mind?"

Liddell shrugged. "Put up the gun and we can talk. I get tongue-tied when somebody's pointing a gun at me."

"You could get dead, too. The same way," Lunfaro growled. "As long as we're getting so chummy, suppose you tell me where it is and save us both a lot of headaches."

"Where what is?"

The muscles bunched along the sides of Lunfaro's mouth while his lips went through the motions of a smile. "The package. The package the old Chink gave you to mind for him. Where is it?"

"Gone. Somebody busted up my office and took it."

Liddell never saw the blow. The flat of the barrel hit him high across the cheek, knocked him to his knees.

"You want to make it tough, peeper, it's okay with me. You'll tell me what I want to know sooner or later. If you're smart it'll be sooner."

Liddell wiped a smear of blood off his cheek with the back of his hand. "What's in that package that's so valuable?"

Lunfaro grinned. "Whatever it is, it's worth a lot of money to some people. Me, I want a lot of money, so I want the package. Where is it, peeper?"

Liddell shook his head. "I told you. Somebody got it from my office." He dodged a kick the gunman aimed at his face. "I'm telling you I haven't got it. Somebody busted into my office, and—"

"You're a liar. I'm the guy that ripped up that rat hole you call an office. It wasn't there."

"You're not the only one after it. Somebody got to it before you did. Somebody who knew his business."

Lunfaro lashed out with his shoe again, but this time Liddell was expecting it. He caught the foot, twisted it with all his strength. Lunfaro hit the floor with a thud and a roar that almost drowned out the sound of the shot.

Liddell was on his feet, jumped on top of the squirming gunman. He forced the wrist of the hand back and away from himself. Lunfaro struggled desperately, tried to bring up his knee. Slowly, he was losing the struggle to bring the gun into play.

The only sound in the apartment was the gasping breaths of the two men on the floor. The perspiration rolled into Liddell's eyes as he slowly but inexorably forced the gun out of Lunfaro's grasp.

Somewhere a door opened and closed. Liddell struggled on, puzzled by the sudden end of Lunfaro's struggling, by the look of triumph on the gunman's face.

Lunfaro relaxed his grip on the gun, let it slide out of his hand. He was looking beyond Liddell, his teeth bared in a wolfish grin of anticipation.

Liddell started to squirm away, heard the swish of the blow as it descended. There was a bright cascade of multicolored lights. He tried to get to his feet, was dully aware of another thud on the back of his head. He managed to get to his knees, wasn't even aware of the third blow, that pitched him face forward, motionless.

A bright burst of pain exploded behind Johnny Liddell's eyeballs when he tried to open his eyes. He fought back a wave of nausea, dragged himself to his knees. His eyes persisted in their reluctance to focus, and the room spun around him dizzily.

He tried to steady himself, found something clutched in his hand. After a moment he was able to identify it as a gun, a .45. Automatically he slid it into his holster, pulled himself to his feet, stood swaying against the side of the couch. As the room stopped spinning and the floor stopped threatening to come up and hit him in the face, he saw Lunfaro.

The gunman was lying on his back, his face frozen in a wolfish grin that bared his teeth. An ominous red stain had spread over the front of his white shirt, spilling off to form a small pool under his outstretched left arm.

Liddell wiped the perspiration off his upper lip with the back of his hand, forced himself to walk over to where the body lay. Lunfaro was dead.

Bits of what had happened started to come back to Liddell. He remembered the struggle with the dead man, the look of triumph on his face, the struggle for Lunfaro's gun, and—

The thought hit him like a dash of cold water. They had been struggling for Lunfaro's gun. Yet he had come to with his own .45 in his hand! How had he gotten the .45? Where was Lunfaro's gun?

Liddell reached in, pulled the .45 from its holster, snapped out the magazine. Three shots had been fired out of it!

He tried desperately to recall what had happened. Had he shot Lunfaro, then passed out?

He knelt beside the dead man, lifted his shirt away from the wounds. From the size of them, it was more than probable that he had been killed with a .45 slug.

Then he had killed Lunfaro! But if he had, who'd hit him? And how had he managed to get his gun?

He straightened up, remembered the girl in the bedroom. She could probably give him the answers he wanted.

The bedroom door was closed. He weaved his way over, shoved the door open with his foot, fanned the room with the .45. The bedroom was smaller than the living room, apparently opened onto a court below. The door to the closet was open as though someone had hurriedly dressed. In the center of the room was a large double bed.

The brunette lay across it, head hanging over the side, a large red stain discoloring the front of her white blouse. Liddell walked over, examined the wound. Again a .45!

Somewhere close a siren wailed. Liddell stiffened, slid the .45 back into his holster. He went back into the living room, quickly wiped off any fingerprints from the doorknob and the armchair where he had been sitting.

From below he could hear the stamp of heavy foot-steps. He bolted the hall door, made for the bedroom. Inside, he closed the door after him, doused the light, headed for the window, raised it.

It was a relatively short drop to the square below. He slid a leg over the sill, caught on with his hands, dropped himself to the courtyard.

Above he could hear sounds of mounting commotion in the apartment he had just quitted. A light flashed on in the bedroom window and a hoarse voice shouted. Liddell made his way cautiously across the courtyard toward a door, apparently leading to an alley.

He had barely reached the courtyard door when a form was silhouetted at the window above. There was a shouted order to "Halt!" Liddell kept going, reached the door, opened it, and slammed it shut behind him. There was a series of sharp snaps and ugly, jagged holes ripped through the wooden door. Liddell kept going.

At the far end of the alley, he came out into a street. A cab cruised by, stopped for his hail. Liddell gave an address on Central Park West, leaned back. From close by came the shriek and wail of sirens.

"Looks like there's plenty of excitement going on some, place around here," the cabby grunted. "Either that or some flattie doing the late shift just don't want nobody else to sleep, neither."

Muggsy opened the door in response to his knock. She was wearing a close-fitting hostess gown of some clingy material that did even more for her than a sweater. Her sleep-heavy eyes widened when she recognized Liddell. He slid by her, closed the door behind him.

Muggsy stabbed automatically at her tousled hair, followed him into the living room. "What time is it?" she demanded.

"Nearly six," Liddell told her. He dropped onto the sofa, jabbed gingerly at the sensitive spots on the top of his head.

"What's happened?" Muggsy wanted to know. Liddell groaned. "I'm in a jam, baby. A real jam."

"Bad?"

Liddell grinned bleakly. "The works. Murder." He slid over, made room for her on the couch. "A beautiful picture with a frame to match and me sitting front row center."

Muggsy shook her head confusedly. "I guess I'm thick. You can't have a murder without someone being dead. Who is?"

"Lunfaro."

The blonde leaned back, made a futile attempt to pull the gown together over her knees, gave it up. "Lunfaro? The one who slugged you at Luigi's?"

Liddell nodded. "That's the one. And everybody in town knows I was after him. Including the police." He reached over to the end table where a bottle of bourbon sat on a tray, caught it by the neck. "Got any glasses, baby? The condemned man wants to drink a hearty breakfast."

Muggsy nodded numbly, went into the kitchenette, returned with some ice and two glasses. She watched while Liddell poured a good-sized slug into each glass. "You didn't, Johnny? I mean, I know it was self-defense if you did. But—you didn't kill him?"

"I don't think so, Muggsy." He took a long pull at the bourbon, ran his fingers through his hair, regretted it. "I don't know."

"What do you mean you don't know, Johnny?"

"I was sapped. While I was fighting with Lunfaro, somebody stepped up behind me and let me have it."

Muggsy dropped down beside him. "Didn't you see who it was?"

Liddell shook his head. "Lunfaro must have. He stopped struggling." He ran the heel of his hand along his chin. "When I came to, he was dead. So was his girl. Both killed with my gun!"

Muggsy Kiely picked a cigarette from the box on the coffee table, lost a fight to keep her hand from shaking as she lit it. "What are we going to do?"

"Lay low. The only way to prove I didn't do it is to get the guy who did." Liddell reached over, took the cigarette from between the blonde's lips, took a deep drag, gave it back. "But the only way I'm going to be able to do that is to stay in the clear."

"But why should they even suspect you, Johnny?"

"Because the job is practically signed with my name. Herlehy knows I was after Lunfaro. The bartender in the club where the girl works knows I went on the make for her tonight. The slugs in them came from my gun."

"But if they don't get the gun to compare with the slugs? They might suspect, but they couldn't prove."

Liddell shook his head. "No such luck. A couple of slugs from my gun are on file at headquarters. The ones they dug out of that hophead Joey in the Nancy Hayes killing."

"But that was self-defense, and—"

Liddell covered her hand with his, squeezed. "I know, baby. But it was a homicide, and the slugs are still on file. All Herlehy has to do is dig them out and compare them with the ones in Lunfaro and I'm cooked."

"What can I do to help, Johnny?"

"What I'm going to ask may compromise you." He grinned.

The blonde made a passable attempt at a grin. "In that case you'll have my pop to answer to." The smile lost some of its vitality. "What do you want me to do?"

"Alibi me for the night. At least for the past few hours. Say from three on. That'll cover me."

"How about the gun?"

Liddell pulled it out of its holster, stared at it. "I'll ditch it, report it as stolen out of the cabinet when my office was busted up." He breathed heavily on the metal surface, examined it closely under the light. "No prints. I didn't expect there would be."

Muggsy took a drink out of her glass, poured some more bourbon over the ice in Liddell's glass. "You know I'll do it, Johnny." She leaned back, studied his profile. "But as long as I'm going to be your partner in crime, don't you think I should know what's going on?"

"I suppose so, baby. But some of this is so top drawer that you can't use it. You can't even hint at it."

"Okay. Just as long as I get the go-ahead before the rest of the gang get the facts. That's our deal?"

Liddell nodded, touched glasses with her, took a deep swallow, put his glass down, and lit a cigarette. "Last night I heard from one of the Dummy's men," he started. "He tipped me off that Lunfaro was at a party at the Hotel Breen in Dream Alley."

Muggsy settled back, folded her feet under her.

"I hot-footed it up there, but by the time I arrived, Lunfaro had been and gone. But the trip wasn't wasted. I met a couple of other friends."

Muggsy waited while he took a deep drag on his cigarette, exhaled through his nostrils. "Who?"

"Ben Cerla and your buddy, Hunt Brin."

Muggsy made an "o" with her lips, nodded for him to go on.

"I think I made a bad mistake up there. I let Brin know I was looking for Lunfaro. I was trying to get some kind of a rise out of him."

"Did he go for it?"

Liddell shook his head. "He's a pretty cold fish. Never even flicked an eyelash."

"I could have told you that," Muggsy nodded. "But suppose he does know you were looking for Lunfaro. Is that bad?"

"Could be. It tips the fact that I had Lunfaro spotted as the gun who gave me the going-over at Luigi's. More important, it tipped the fact that I was hep to the tie-up between Brin, Cerla, and Lunfaro."

Muggsy chewed on the end of a fingernail, considered it. "You think Brin went over and killed Lunfaro to shut him up?" She gave it another minute, then shook her head. "Maybe I'm wrong, but I can't see Hunt as a killer.

Peddling marijuana to school kids, rigging roulette wheels, or romancing an old dowager out of her bond coupons, yes. But not a killer."

"Maybe Brin isn't the top man, baby. Maybe he's just a cog."

"I could buy that faster than Brin as a killer," Muggsy assented.

Liddell got up from the couch, walked over to the windows facing out over Central Park. He stared down at the lights that flickered palely in the dawn. "Look, Muggsy, I have no right to tell you this. On the other hand, I have no right to let you get mixed up in this thing unless I do." He walked back to the couch, dropped down beside her. "This thing is bigger than rigging roulette wheels, bigger even than murder."

"I gathered that," she told him dryly. "You're not going out getting yourself on the wrong end of a murder rap for nothing. Tell mamma."

"Remember the boys who came up to the office after Hong left? The ones with the search warrant?"

Muggsy nodded.

"I saw them again last night," Liddell told her.

"The ones that posed as federal men?"

Liddell nodded. "They were federal men. That was a bona fide search warrant."

"What? I thought you said Byers at Treasury said he never heard of you or Hong or the package or anything else?"

Liddell nodded, chain-lit another cigarette. "He did. But he was under orders to cover up. Hong was an undercover federal agent."

Muggsy leaned back limply. "Go on."

Liddell grinned. "That's not all. It gets screwier as it goes along, believe me." He pinched his nostrils between thumb and forefinger. "Remember the hustler I told you about? The bleached-blond pre-war model that had a flat right under Hong's?"

"I think so. What about her?"

"She was at Hunt Brin's party last night, all decked out in a fancy gown and a new hair-do. She was acting as hostess and serving drinks, no less."

"Now wait a minute, Johnny. G-men who aren't G-men, but really are G-men I can swallow. Now you're asking me to believe that a broken-down old hustler travels with Hunt Brin's café-society crowd. Why, a professional wouldn't have a chance with all the amateur competition in that crowd."

"Maybe it isn't business." Liddell held up a finger. "Look at it this way. Goldy's been in the racket ten, fifteen years as far as I can figure. Check?"

Muggsy nodded. "If you say so."

"Okay. Now think back to those clippings we had on Ben Cerla. About ten years or so ago, he had all the vice protection in this town sewed up tight. So, to a gal like Goldy, he was really a big wheel, knew his way around, knew the right people." He held out his cigarette, let the girl light hers from it. "Now, suppose she gets a red-hot idea for a big take. Who do you think would be the first one she'd look up to cut in on it?"

Muggsy worried her lower lip between her teeth. "Sounds okay. But where does Brin come in?"

"Suppose the deal Goldy brings to Cerla is out of his class. Suppose he needs a good front with proper con- tacts? Who pops into his mind? His old buddy and partner, Hunt Brin!" Liddell waited for an argument, got none. "They go into business together, cut the take three ways. Goldy provides the know-how in Chinatown. After all, she knows her way around like nobody else down there. Cerla provides the muscle. Brin provides the front. All nice and neat."

"Narcotics?" Muggsy guessed.

"Bigger than that. A lot bigger," Liddell told her. "They're shaking down the rich Chinese for ransom."

"Ransom? You mean kidnaping? There's none been reported."

Liddell grinned bleakly. "Not here. The kidnapping is going on in parts of occupied China. Relatives of rich Chinese in this country are grabbed, and unless the rich American relatives shell out, the hostages are liquidated."

"You think that's Hunt Brin's new racket?"

Liddell nodded. "Goldy fingers the prospects. She knows who has how much over here and where their relatives are. She fingers the ones to be taken, passes the information along to Cerla, and Brin gets it through to the Chinese warlords."

Muggsy whistled noiselessly. "That is a big deal. You're trying to crack that racket? That's out of your class, Johnny. That's international stuff."

"Maybe. But I'm going to either crack it or die trying."

"That doesn't sound too hard to do. Not the way these boys play."

CHAPTER ELEVEN

INSPECTOR HERLEHY SAT behind the battered old desk in his office, and glared at Johnny Liddell and Muggsy Kiely. "I'd probably be doing you and the public a favor if I locked you up and threw the key away," he growled at Liddell. "You're as irresponsible as a junior-grade moron driving a hot rod, and twice as fatal."

Johnny Liddell squirmed uncomfortably on the hardwood chair. "You've got me all wrong, inspector. I tell you I didn't kill Lunfaro. You can't make it stick and you know it."

Herlehy chomped indignantly on the wad of gum. "Maybe not, but I sure as hell could make a good stab at it." He swung around, regarded Muggsy Kiely from under bushy eyebrows. "You still stick to your story that Liddell spent the night with you?"

Muggsy dropped her eyes, examined the lacquer finish on her fingernails. "He dropped by at about two-thirty or three for a nightcap, and we didn't notice how the time was flying." She looked up. "It was morning before we knew it."

"*Lovely,*" Herlehy snorted. He got up from his chair, stamped across the room to the water cooler, took a drink. "I'm warning you, Liddell. If I hang this one on you, I'm going to make it stick. I told you you didn't have a hunting-license for Lunfaro, and I meant it. Whether he deserved killing or not, you won't get away with it."

"And if I can prove I didn't kill him?"

Herlehy came back to the desk, stood braced in front of Liddell. "How?"

"By getting the guy who did."

Herlehy sneered. "You do that, Liddell. You bring him in and I'll personally buy you a new forty-five to take the place of the one you so conveniently lost."

"I didn't lose it. Whoever busted into my office stole it," Liddell corrected him. "I reported it first thing this morning." He grinned up at Herlehy. "Besides, I'd rather have my old gun back if you happen to find it."

"If we happen to find it, I have a hunch you won't be having any further use for guns," Herlehy growled.

There was a knock on the door; the inspector snapped a "Come in." A tall man in civilian clothes, which failed completely to erase the label Cop, walked in and saluted.

"I'm Stack, inspector. I got orders from the precinct to report to you this morning."

Herlehy nodded briefly. "You were in the squad car that answered the call in that double killing early this morning?"

The man in plain clothes nodded. "Yes, sir."

"The report says you saw the killer escaping through the courtyard, threw a couple shots after him. Take a look at this man," he indicated Liddell with a toss of his head. "This him?"

The big man turned a pair of cold, impersonal eyes on Liddell, studied him, finally shook his head. "I couldn't say yes, inspector. It wasn't light yet, and I was two stories above him. I only saw the man for a few minutes before he ducked through the door into the alley." He returned his gaze to Liddell. "Could be. Maybe not."

Herlehy nodded his head impatiently. "Okay, Stack. Thanks for coming over." He waited until the man had closed the door behind him. "Your luck's still holding, Liddell."

Liddell grinned. "I don't get it, inspector. Why suspect me? I'm completely in the clear."

Herlehy grinned nastily. "There are men frying in the death house who have a better out than yours. You lost your gun, the one that killed the two people. You say. You were with Muggsy at the time of the killing. She says. You're both cockeyed liars. I say."

"You sound like you don't believe my story, inspector," Muggsy pouted.

"Believe your story? Putting yourself in a position like that just to give this trigger-happy shamus an alibi? If I was your father—"

"As a representative of the *Advance*, would you like to make the statement that you're not satisfied with Johnny Liddell's alibi and that he is a suspect in the murder?" Muggsy cut in.

Herlehy glared at her. "Not right now. If it's true, I don't want to rip your reputation to shreds. If it's not true, I don't want to look like a fool by letting him roam the streets."

Muggsy pursed her lips. "I know just what you mean, inspector."

"I thought you would," Herlehy growled. He turned his back, walked around the desk. "Now, get out of here, both of you, before I change my mind and toss you both in the clink for obstructing justice."

The taxi dropped Johnny Liddell and Muggsy Kiely at the corner of Park Row and Worth. Liddell pointed out the house in which the old Chinese had been murdered.

"You'd better stay out here, Muggs. I won't be long. I just want a few words with Goldy."

Muggsy Kiely looked around her, wrinkled her nose at the old derelicts sprawled out full length on the sidewalks, the staggering wrecks that zigzagged from curb to building line and back.

"I don't know what it's like in there, but it can't be any worse than out here." She shook her head. "I'm coming in with you."

Liddell started to argue, decided he couldn't win, shrugged his shoulders. "It may be unpleasant, if we're lucky. If we're not it may be damn dangerous." He consulted his watch. "Why don't you hop a cab and go on down to the paper? I'll check you later."

Muggsy shook her head. "No soap, Liddell. I can't look my poor old pop in the eye until the blemish on my character has been removed." She grinned. "We're partners in this deal, my boy, and partners share everything, including the risks. Lead on."

Liddell led the way up the small stoop, through the pornographically decorated vestibule, and into the malodorous hall. Muggsy kept close to him until he reached Goldy's door.

"I'll go in first. If it's okay, you can follow," he whispered.

Muggsy started to protest, was silenced by his finger on his lips. She snorted her complaint, but remained silent.

Liddell knocked, waited for a response. There was no sound from inside the apartment. He knocked again, got no reply.

"Maybe they killed her, too," Muggsy whispered. "We better call the police."

Liddell tried the knob, found it locked. He was feeling through his pockets for a bunch of keys when a rough hand fell on Muggsy's arm. Her scream deafened him momentarily, but Liddell swung around, hand streaking for his shoulder holster.

An old man in a dingy-colored undershirt stood regarding Muggsy with a complete lack of interest. "Didn't mean to scare you, lady," he assured her placidly. He looked from her to Liddell, let an appraising gaze run up and down the private detective. "Looking for Goldy, mister?"

Liddell nodded, dropped his hand to his side. "Yeah."

The old man ran his tongue over toothless gums, sucked at them noisily. "She ain't here."

"Know when she'll be back?"

The old man shook his head. "She ain't coming back. Pulled out for good, looks like."

Liddell swore under his breath. "Know where I can get in touch with her?"

The old man looked him up and down incuriously. "Nope. Moved out early this morning. Middle of the night, you might say."

Liddell turned, stared at the locked door. "Haven't got a key to this, have you? I'd like to look around."

The old man ran the sleeve of his undershirt under his nose, shook his head. "Ain't got no right to let anybody in. Not less you was figuring on renting." He leered at Muggsy. "Make a mighty fine honeymoon spot for a couple."

Muggsy shuddered. "I'll bet."

"What's the rent?" Liddell wanted to know.

The old man pursed slack lips, stared up at the ceiling. "Thirty-five a month."

Liddell pulled out his wallet, fumbled in it, came up with a five. "How about a one-hour option?"

The old man bared toothless gums in a grin. "Why not?" He stuck his broom under his arm, brought an old-fashioned key from his pants pocket, unlocked the door, pushed it open. "You ain't figuring on doing any damage?"

Liddell looked in, shook his head. "Just figuring on taking a look around."

The old man nodded contentedly, tossed the broom toward the cellar staircase, started for the front door.

Inside the apartment, Liddell located the hall light he had seen Goldy put on during his first visit. He led the way to the kitchen, made a brief survey of the bedroom and the old-fashioned bathroom.

"She's gone, all right," he growled. "I didn't think she spotted me last night, but she must have."

Methodically, they set about searching every inch of the flat for some clue to the woman's destination. They drew a complete blank. The packing had been hurried but efficient.

Liddell was ready to call it a day, about to admit complete failure, when, as a matter of routine, he examined the sink in the bathroom. Attached to the underside by strips of adhesive was a photograph. He ripped it loose, brought it out under the hall light.

It was a picture of an elderly Chinese in military uniform. Liddell recognized it immediately as a photograph of Hong, the man who had left the package in his office, later died painfully in the apartment directly above the one in which they were now standing.

Muggsy peered curiously over his shoulder, took the picture out of Liddell's hand, held it under the light.

"Hong?" she guessed.

Liddell nodded.

Muggsy turned it over, found no notation on the back, handed it to Liddell. "What's it doing here?"

"Acting as the old man's death warrant."

"What do you mean?"

Liddell stuck the picture in his breast pocket. "Somehow the gang got word that an undercover agent was going to get planted in their midst. The picture was sent to them so they'd spot him when he arrived." He took a last look around, growled. "The poor old guy was a sitting duck. He never had a chance."

"If they knew him from the minute he arrived, why did they wait so long to kill him?" Muggsy asked.

Liddell shrugged. "Who knows? Maybe they wanted to see who his contact was. Maybe the picture didn't get here until recently. My guess is they wanted to see who he turned his reports in to."

Muggsy nodded, did a slow double take. "Wait a minute. That means you. They probably followed him to your place. They probably think you're the one who planted him here."

Liddell grinned glumly. "That's probably why they're so anxious to plant me."

Muggsy shuddered, looked around apprehensively. "What about the woman who lived here? Goldy?"

"In it up to her unwashed neck."

"What are we going to do?"

Liddell reached up, snapped off the light. "First we're going to get out of here. Sooner or later she's going to remember where she left this thing and send for it."

"Maybe she'll come back herself."

Liddell shook his head. "She probably sent a messenger to do her packing in the first place. That's why this was overlooked. She'll probably send the same one back, and we don't want to be here when he arrives."

Outside on the street, Liddell hailed a cab, gave the driver the address of the *Advance*, leaned back against the cushions.

"I got news for you, Johnny," Muggsy told him. "If you're figuring on dropping me off at the office, no soap. I'm sticking along."

Liddell fumbled for his cigarettes, found himself out, took the girl's purse, ransacked it to come up with a pack. "Not this time, Muggs. I've got some straight talking to do, and I do it best without witnesses." He stuck a cigarette in the corner of his mouth, lit it, dropped his voice. "I want you some place where I can keep in touch. I may need help, and fast, and I want somebody in a position to get it to me when I yell."

"Where will you be?"

"Having a little talk with friend Brin."

Muggsy lifted the cigarette from between his lips, took a deep drag. "You shouldn't go there alone. Particularly if he's the one you think killed Lunfaro."

"I'm not going alone. I'm taking old Betsy with me, and she's plenty of company." He tapped at his shoulder holster, remembered belatedly it was empty, snapped his fingers. "Where'd you hide my gun?"

"You said it was dangerous to carry it."

"It'd be more dangerous not to right now. Where is it?"

Muggsy sighed, shrugged. "You know what you're doing—I hope. It's under the cushion of the chaise longue in my bedroom." She stared forlornly at the front facade of the *Advance* office as the cab skidded to a stop at the curb. "What am I suppose to do here besides bite my nails?"

Liddell grinned. "It's not that tough, baby. While I'm on my way uptown to your place, suppose you dig around and find out where Brin holes out. I'll call you from your apartment."

Muggsy nodded, started to get out. "How'll you get in?"

"That's right. You'd better give me a key."

Muggsy uttered a fake groan. "Now I am a lost woman. First he spends the night with me, advertises it all over town. Now I give him a key." She turned to stare down the leer of the cabby, found the keys in her purse, tossed them to Liddell. "Have supper ready when I get home." She slammed the cab door, clicked her high heels across the pavement to the building.

Johnny Liddell let himself into Muggsy Kiely's apartment with her key, stood in the entrance hall for a moment, strained his ears, heard no evidence of any other occupancy. He walked directly through the living room to the bedroom beyond, pulled back the cushion of the chaise longue, retrieved his .45. He pulled out the magazine, satisfied himself it still contained shells, slipped it into his holster.

In the kitchen, he filled a glass with ice cubes, spilled some bourbon into it, carried it into the living room to the telephone. He dialed his office, waited until the metallic voice informed him. "Johnny Liddell's office."

"Hello, Pinky," he greeted the receptionist. "This is Liddell."

He could hear the sharp intake of breath. "Where are you? I've been trying to reach you every place. At your hotel they said you didn't come home all night." There was a sharp note of suspicion in her voice.

"I'm surprised at you," he chided. "You know I never sleep when I'm on a case. After all, I've got a client, don't forget."

"Don't you forget it," the receiver snapped back. "Your client's been trying to reach you all morning. He wants you to call him as soon as you can."

"Jimmy Kaiming?"

"Yeah. Why? How many clients you got?"

Liddell took a sip from his glass. "How's the office?"

"Looks like a batch of woodpeckers and some gophers held a marathon contest here, but I've got most of the papers picked up." She sighed. "But that pretty desk of yours will never be the same."

"I saw it. I was in there last night." He consulted his watch. "I've got some things to do. If I can't get back there, I'll check in by phone at six. Leave any important messages with the answering service."

There was a sniff over the wire that could have meant anything, then the line went dead. Liddell scowled at the receiver, dropped it back on its cradle. He dialed another number, waited until the operator at the *Advance* answered, asked for Muggsy Kiely.

Muggsy's voice came through after a minute. "Johnny?"

"Yeah. Get that information for me?"

"I think I have what you want. I just called you there and I got a busy signal."

Liddell grinned. "I called my office."

"What's the matter?" the receiver snapped. "Lonesome for your redhead? As long as it's my phone, you might have called me first."

"Relax, baby, I've got to check in sometime, don't I? What've you got on Brin?"

"Hunt Brin's registered at the Carter House," the receiver told him coldly. "It's right across the Park from my place, On Fifth."

Liddell nodded. "I know the place. Anything else in Brin's file I ought to know?"

"Nothing too interesting," Muggsy's voice trailed off. "I have his file right in front of me. The usual café-society drool, a few clips and cross-references on the Ben Cerla mess. Nothing else."

"Okay, I'm on my way."

A note of anxiety crept into Muggsy's voice. "I've been thinking, Johnny, it's crazy to see Brin. What can he tell you?"

Liddell shrugged. "Who knows? Goldy seems to be the key to this whole mess. Brin knows her well enough to use her as a hostess. Maybe I can persuade him to tell me where to find her."

"All right, Johnny," the receiver told him. "But there are two principals dead in this case already. Just remember what they always say about death coming in threes."

CHAPTER TWELVE

THE LOBBY OF THE CARTER HOUSE was furnished in modernistic style, with brightly colored couches and chrome chairs and tables complementing the soft, restful pastel carpeting. Johnny Liddell crossed the lobby, approached the impeccably dressed man behind the desk.

"Mr. Brin, please."

The man behind the desk raised heavy-lidded eyes from a critical examination of the carnation in his button hole. "Mr. Huntington Brin?"

"Yeah. What room's he in?"

"Mr. Huntington Brin has the penthouse, sir." There was a hurt tone in his voice, the half-closed eyes were reproachful. "The Carter House does not rent rooms. Apartments and suites only." He adjusted the edge of a cuff that peeked from the end of his sleeve. "I'm afraid we cannot disturb Mr. Brin. He never rises before three."

"I can," Liddell told him. He spun on his heel, headed for the bank of elevators. He gave no sign that he had caught the signal that passed between the clerk and one of the housemen.

A waiting elevator holding an elderly lady with startling blue hair and a gray-haired man who was evidently uncomfortable with the corset he was wearing slammed its doors and started upward as Liddell approached. The uniformed starter ushered Liddell to another elevator, waited while a tall, tired-looking man stepped in, signaled for it to go up.

"Penthouse," Liddell told the operator.

"Fifth." The tired-looking man sighed.

The cage jerked to a stop at the fifth floor, the door slid open. Two men in business suits stood waiting. The tall, tired-looking man tapped Liddell on the shoulder. "We get off here, mister."

"You build your penthouses low in this place," Liddell commented. "I wanted to go to the penthouse."

"We get off here," the tired man repeated.

Liddell looked from his face to the elevator operator to the two waiting men. "You talked me into it." He shrugged.

They walked down the heavily carpeted hall to a door that said *Executive Offices* in gold leaf. The tired-looking man rapped, opened the door, stood aside for Liddell.

The restful *decor* of the lobby had been carried over into the executive offices. Everything in the room seemed to blend restfully with the exception of the man behind the desk. His chair was tilted back against the wall, the heel of one tremendous shoe was hooked on the corner of the highly polished desk, a cigar was clenched between his teeth. He stared at Liddell coldly.

"This him?" he growled to the tired-looking man.

The man nodded. "Picked him up at the elevator. Got an SOS from the pantywaist at the desk."

The man behind the desk rolled the cigar from one corner of his mouth to the other. "He told me over the phone all about it." He nodded for the three men to leave. "What's it all about, friend?" he asked when the door had closed behind the other three.

"You tell me. All I did was ask to see Hunt Brin and right away I get a military escort. What's the idea?"

The man behind the desk pulled the cigar from between his teeth, studied the soggy end, licked a loose leaf back into position. "No idea, friend." He raised his eyes to Liddell. "It just happens I'm his social secretary. I gotta find out what you want to see him about."

Liddell stared at the man for a moment, then grinned. "You're Kenneally."

The cold eyes of the man behind the desk narrowed. He jammed the cigar back between his teeth, dropped his feet from the desk, leaned forward. "How'd you know my name?"

Liddell dropped into a chair at the far side of the desk, leaned back. "Inspector's Office, Homicide Division. Back maybe eight, ten years. Right?"

Kenneally chewed on the end of the cigar. "I know all about me, friend. You're the one I don't know about."

"Name's Liddell, Johnny Liddell. Back in your day I worked out of the Acme office here in town."

The man behind the desk pounded it with the flat of his hand, looked disgusted. "I thought you looked familiar. Liddell, eh?" He peered at him intently. "Sure. Now, I make you." He leaned back in his chair, massaged the side of his jaw with the heel of his hand. "That ain't so good. A shamus wanting to see one of our guests. What's the beef?"

Liddell shrugged. "Why does there have to be a beef? All I want is some conversation."

"Conversation? No trouble?"

"No trouble," Liddell assured him.

"Then why're you heeled?" Kenneally indicated the bulge in Liddell's breast pocket with the soggy end of his cigar.

"Habit. I'd feel undressed without it."

Kenneally nodded, seemed satisfied. "Suppose Brin doesn't want conversation?"

Liddell grinned humorlessly. "I think he will. Why don't you ask him? Tell him Inspector Herlehy knows I'm here and that we both think it's better for Brin to talk to me than to take a trip downtown."

The man behind the desk plucked at his lower lip. "Like that?"

"Like that."

"How do I know you're not bluffing, Liddell?"

Liddell shrugged. "You don't. But this much you do know. If I get to talk to Brin there won't be a squad of harness bulls tramping through the lobby scaring hell out of the hothouse pansies you cultivate in this place. And believe me, the management isn't going to be very grateful if you stop me and Herlehy and his boys do have to move in."

Kenneally tried to stare him down through slitted eyelids, gave up, reached for the phone. After a moment of mumbled conversation he slammed the receiver back on the hook, nodded. "Brin will see you." He jammed the ragged end of the cigar back between his teeth, ground it savagely. "Just remember—no trouble."

The man who opened the door to Brin's apartment was one of the two guards Hunt Brin had had stationed at the party at the Hotel Breen. He swung the door open wide in response to Liddell's knock, stepped aside so Liddell would have to precede him into the room.

"Mr. Brin will see you in there," he nodded toward an open doorway with his head.

As Liddell stepped past him, the guard closed the door, fell in behind him. Liddell felt the sharp snout of a gun poke into his back.

"One thing, first, Liddell," the guard told him in flat tones. "The house dick says you're heeled. Mr. Brin is very nervous about firearms." Liddell made no move as the man slid his hand into his jacket, came up with his .45, then patted the other pockets. "Okay, now let's go."

Hunt Brin was sprawled on an oversized couch against the far wall of the inner room. He was wearing a bright, blue dressing gown, a yellow ascot-type scarf knotted at his open neck. He didn't bother to get up as Liddell walked in.

"Well, so we meet again, Liddell." The lazy smile was pasted back on his face.

"Monotonous, isn't it?" Liddell agreed.

Brin shrugged. "It's your choice, you know." He waved negligently to a chair. "Make yourself comfortable." The cold blue chips of his eyes followed Liddell across the room to a barrel chair. "I take it this is a social call?"

The guard snorted, held up the .45. "Here's his calling card." He tossed it down on the couch next to the blond man. "The house dick tipped me off."

"Very efficient system we have in this hotel, eh, Liddell?" Brin smiled. He picked up the .45 hefted it in the palm of his hand. "A nice weapon."

"I thought you were nervous with firearms," Liddell grunted.

"Only when they're in somebody else's hands. Now, what was it you wanted to talk about, Liddell?"

"Lunfaro."

A look of annoyance clouded Brin's eyes, passed quickly. "We discussed this friend of yours last night, Liddell, and—"

131

"Lunfaro's dead, Brin," Liddell told him. There was no mistaking the shocked surprise on the blond man's face. He made a creditable effort at recovery, dropped his eyes, made a production of selecting a cigarette and lighting it. He couldn't control the shake of his hand.

"Then you did find him last night?" His eyes rolled up, pasted themselves on Liddell.

"I found him, all right. So did a killer who was afraid he might talk too much."

Brin took a long drag, blew a stream of blue-white smoke ceiling ward, and asked, "Talking? About what?"

Liddell shrugged. "Lots of things. Ben Cerla, you. The old blond hustler from Chinatown—"

The cigarette stopped halfway to Brin's mouth. "The what?"

"Goldy. The old bag from Chinatown you were using as a hostess at your wing-ding last night."

Brin's laugh sounded forced. "You must have picked up one of the butts from a tray last night. You ought to stick to tobacco."

"I suppose you know she pulled out of her Chinatown flat last night, leaving no forwarding address. She must have seen me and realized I recognized her. I want to talk to her, Brin. Where is she?"

"I just told you I don't know what you're talking about."

"You're a liar," Liddell growled.

The guard walked over to where Liddell sat, caught him by the lapels, dragged him to his feet. Liddell broke the man's hold with a quick upward and outward fling of his hands, smashed the tip of his toe into the guard's instep. The man roared with pain, dropped his guard. Liddell sank his left into the other man's middle, chopped down against the side of his jaw with a right. The guard hit the floor without a sound, lay there.

"Very pretty." Hunt Brin applauded. His right hand held Liddell's gun, its snout pointed unwaveringly at the detective's midsection. "Very pretty indeed." His eyes flicked to the unconscious man at Liddell's feet. "Not that Tim will appreciate it. He rather fancies himself as pretty tough, you know." His eyes rolled up to Liddell. "Jujitsu?"

"Judo, actually. You ought to tell him he's a wide-open sucker for a left, incidentally."

"I'll tell him," Brin promised solemnly. He waved Liddell back to the chair with the snout of the .45. "Now, while we're waiting for Tim to rejoin us, suppose you tell me what you're really after."

"Goldy."

Hunt Brin sighed. "Last night it was Lunfaro. Today he's dead. Now it's this Goldy. What's it all about, Liddell?"

"Murder."

"Whose?"

Liddell disregarded the gun, walked over to a glass-topped coffee table, helped himself to a cigarette. "A client of mine. A little Chink named Hong."

Brin watched Liddell light the cigarette, flip the spent match at an ashtray. "What's this Goldy got to do with that?"

"That's what I want to ask her. She lived downstairs from the old guy."

Brin nodded. "I see. Why was he killed?"

Liddell drew deeply on the cigarette, exhaled through his nostrils. "Who knows? My guess is that he was trying to muscle into Gee Faw." He regarded the glowing end of the cigarette, flicked an invisible film of ash from its end.

"Maybe some of the boys running the game wouldn't like that."

"Like Ben Cerla, for instance?" Brin asked softly.

"Could be."

Hunt Brin hefted the .45 in his hand, stroked the barrel. "And you've heard that Cerla and I were once partners. That it?"

Liddell nodded. "I heard you were tied up with Cerla in other gambling rackets. It did occur to me you might be in Gee Faw with him."

"So what you're really here for is because you think I might have had something to do with this little Chink's murder."

"Did you?"

The lazy smile was back on the blond man's face. "I never heard of him until you just mentioned his name. I don't know your charming friend Goldy and I've never heard of Lunfaro. As for Cerla," he shrugged, "as far as I know he runs a legitimate restaurant in Chinatown."

"And you?"

"Just a guy who doesn't like to be annoyed." He nodded to the man on the floor who was beginning to groan his way back to consciousness. "I think you'd better get along before Tim comes to. I'd hate to have my furniture smashed."

"You haven't been much help," Liddell told him ruefully.

Brin smiled. "I didn't intend to be." He motioned to the door with the gun. "I'd run along if I were you."

Liddell shrugged, walked to the door. "And my gun?"

"You're welcome to it." He handed it over, barrel first. Liddell took it by the barrel between thumb and forefinger, slid it into his holster.

Brin opened the door. Outside was Kenneally, the house detective. He looked from Brin to Liddell, then to the unconscious man on the floor inside the apartment.

"Everything okay, Mr. Brin?" he asked.

Brin nodded, his eyes on Liddell. "Yes, Kenneally. Everything's quite okay."

Liddell walked down the hall, heard the door close behind him. He was almost to the elevator when Kenneally caught him by the arm, swung him around. "I thought you said no rough stuff, Liddell."

"Rough stuff? You heard what the man said, Kenneally. Everything was okay. We're pals. Real pals."

"How about the guy stretched out on the floor?" the house detective growled.

"Him? Oh, he just knocked himself out making me feel at home."

CHAPTER THIRTEEN

JOHNNY LIDDELL WALKED into the restaurant, looked around. Muggsy Kiely waved from a back booth. He walked through the closely packed tables, slid in beside her.

"What's happened, Johnny?" she demanded breathlessly. "I got your message to meet here. I've been on pins and needles ever since."

"I want you to do something for me, Muggs," Liddell told her. "Something I can't do myself."

"What is it?"

"I want you to deliver a package to Inspector Herlehy for me."

Muggsy's face dropped. "That's what the hurry-up call was all about?"

"That's all for now, but things are really beginning to break wide open," Liddell assured her. He waited until the waitress had accepted his order for a cup of coffee and had gone. "Wide open."

"Did you see Brin?" Muggsy asked.

"I saw him, and I gave him plenty to think about."

"Did he tell you what you wanted to know? About Goldy, I mean."

Liddell shook his head. "Not a word. He's a hard boy. Hard as glass."

"That's just ducky. You sure must have thrown a scare into him. You didn't get a thing. All you did was tip off what little you do know," Muggsy flared. The waitress slopped two cups of coffee in front of them, retired to the kitchen. "You think it's news that he's as hard as glass? That's why they've never been able to pin anything on him!"

Liddell nodded, sipped at his coffee. "I know, I know. Ever see glass when it does break? It smashes into a million pieces. That's the way Brin will break."

"How are you going to make him break?"

Liddell winked. "You'll see, baby. When he's ready to break, he'll come looking for us. We won't have to go looking for him."

"You're holding out on me, Johnny," Muggsy accused.

Liddell produced a handkerchief-wrapped package from his jacket pocket. "Just see to it that Herlehy gets this. Tell him to check it for fingerprints and to check it against the slugs they took out of Lunfaro."

Muggsy's eyes widened. "It's your gun!"

Liddell nodded, sipped at his coffee. "It's a persuader. In more ways than one."

"You're crazy, Johnny," the girl gasped. "This is all they need to pin Lunfaro's murder on you. You know Herlehy's turning the town upside down looking for this gun."

"Sure. That's why we're giving it to him. We're cooperating with the police. Just see to it he gets the gun, baby. Then let's see what happens."

Muggsy slipped the gun gingerly into her envelope bag. "What are you going to be doing while I'm signing your warrant?"

"I've got to check in with my client. My office tells me he's been trying to reach me all day." He looked at his watch. "It's almost three, I'll check you about six at the paper. Okay?"

"Where do I tell Herlehy I got this thing?" Muggsy wanted to know.

"Tell him that I gave it to you and that I'll explain everything when I talk to him." He finished his coffee, dropped a handful of change on the table. "Get it over to headquarters as fast as you can, will you, Muggs? We haven't got too much time if we're going to wrap this up right." He picked up a dime from the table. " Wait here, I'm going to call Kaiming and tell him I'm on my way down."

Muggsy Kiely was still chewing on her lower lip when Liddell returned to the table. "Kaiming's out. Won't be back until late, I'll have to see him then."

"You still want me to take this to Herlehy?" Muggsy held up her bag. "Or do you want to take it as long as you can't see Kaiming?"

"You take it," Liddell told her. "If I do, he'd waste too much time asking me about it and a lot of other un- necessary stuff. I don't want to have to talk to him until he's got the fingerprint and ballistics report."

"Where'll you be in case I want to reach you?"

Liddell grinned. "The last place in town anybody would think of looking for me. In my office."

Liddell sat with his desk chair tilted back, staring out the window into Bryant Park twelve stories below. He helped himself to a slug of bourbon out of the bottle in the bottom drawer, emptied the paper cup, tossed it at the wastebasket. He consulted his watch, frowned at the time. Almost seven. He reached for the telephone, dialed police headquarters. When the male operator answered, Liddell asked for Inspector Herlehy, gave his name.

Herlehy was on the line in a flash. "Liddell?" he roared across the wire. "Where the hell are you?"

"In my office, inspector," Liddell told him mildly. "Why?"

"You know damn well why. Where did you get that gun you sent over here this afternoon?"

Liddell grinned. "That was my gun. The one I reported stolen when my office was wrecked last night, and—"

"Quit stalling," the receiver barked. "You know what I mean. Where did you get it today?"

"Took it away from a guy who tried to jump me this morning."

"What guy?"

Liddell shrugged. "I don't know. He got away. That's why I sent the gun over to you for examination. I thought you might find something that would help. Did you?"

The receiver snorted. "We found plenty. It was the gun that killed Lunfaro, all right. And we got the prints on it pegged."

"Good. Whose were they?"

"I don't know if I should tell you," the receiver hesitated. "I've got a hunch you're not coming clean with me. What's going on, Liddell?"

"Whose prints, inspector?" Liddell persisted.

"Brin's. Hunt Brin's." The voice on the other end of the wire calmed down a trifle. "Funny thing. You go hunting Lunfaro, he turns up dead. You go out after Brin, his prints turn up on a murder gun. You're worse than an epidemic."

"Something wrong with the prints, inspector?" Liddell asked.

"No," Herlehy conceded glumly. "Not a thing. Brin, held the gun in his hand, all right, and he had his finger on the trigger. There were three shots fired from it and they turned up in Lunfaro and the Ryan girl. The prints are perfect, Liddell. So perfect I'd give a week's salary to know how you managed it."

"What's Brin got to say, inspector?"

Herlehy swore fervently. "He's skipped. We put a wanted order out on the wire about five. That turncoat harness bull Kenneally must have tipped Brin. He never showed back to his apartment." A wheedling note entered the inspector's voice. "You wouldn't have any idea of where he might be, Liddell?"

"How would I know, inspector?"

"You were the last one to see him today," the receiver accused. "This whole mess smells to high heaven. I hope for your sake your skirts are clean, Liddell."

Liddell grinned. "I'm as innocent as a new-born babe. By the way, inspector, when do I get my gun back?"

"You don't. It's impounded as evidence!" The receiver slammed in Liddell's ear. He grinned wryly, returned the instrument to its cradle, leaned back, stared out over 42nd Street.

The wanted order on Hunt Brin had gone out hours ago. The chances were that Brin already knew he was wanted. That meant the case was going into the stretch. Liddell grinned glumly, wondered if he'd live long enough to see it come in under the wire.

Bryant Park across the street was almost dark. Liddell had failed to put on the lights in the office, sat in semi-darkness, staring out onto the city below.

The phone started to jangle impatiently on the desk behind him. Liddell let it ring three times, picked it up.

The voice on the other end was low, unidentifiable. "Liddell?"

"That's right. Where are you, Brin?"

There was a slight pause. "So you were expecting me to call, eh? Well, you won't be disappointed, peeper, I'm coming for you."

Liddell nodded. "That's what I'm waiting for. Now maybe we can have that talk I suggested this afternoon."

"I hear it's tough to do any talking with a hole in your head. You think I'm standing still for this frame?"

Liddell laughed into the mouthpiece. "That's real smart. Have me bumped off. That'll put you in the soup for real. Get smart. Let's deal."

"What've you got to deal with, peeper?"

Liddell shrugged. "Your hide. I'm the only one that knows how you were framed with my gun. I could keep you out of the hot seat."

The voice on the other end became hesitant. "Go on."

"You tell me what I want to know and I'll take you off the hook on the gun. If anything happens to me, there's nothing that can keep you from frying." Liddell chuckled. "You may not know it, but you've got a pretty big stake in me. You'd better start hoping I don't even catch cold."

"How do I know I can trust you?" The metallic voice was undecided. "How do I know this isn't another fast one like the gun?"

"I want to see Goldy. I'm not interested in putting you on the spot." He could hear the heavy breathing of the man on the other end of the phone. "Why cover for somebody else? Sure, by holding out on me, you'll be a hero to them—a well-cooked hero. Well?"

"You know Marty's on Waverly Place in the Village?"

"I can find it."

"Meet me there in an hour. Come alone and don't try anything. They're getting set to tag me for a killing I didn't do. Cross me and I'll give them a good reason."

The receiver clicked in his ear. Liddell returned it to his desk. He checked his watch, walked over to the cupboard against the wall, selected a snub-nosed .38 from his arsenal, slid it into his jacket pocket.

The neon sign drenched the sidewalks with a dull-red glow. It flickered fitfully in the drizzle, announced to the public: *Marty's Place*. The door was three steps up from Waverly Place, opened into a small vestibule that had been converted into a checkroom. A heavily painted blonde presided over the coats hanging on the wall. It required a second look to identify the "girl" as a man.

Johnny Liddell walked through into a huge room that served as a combination barroom and dance floor. The lights were low, orange-colored, spilled deep shadows all over the place. A small bar was set against the far wall, was empty except for two Marines and a heavy-set man in drag.

Liddell ambled over, leaned on the bar. The bartender was heavy, fleshy. His eyes were almost hidden behind their huge pouches, his lips were a thick, wet smear. But at least he affected pants.

"Bourbon and water," Liddell told him.

The bartender pushed a thick-bottomed jigger across the bar with a pudgy, dimpled hand, reached for a bottle. Liddell shoved back the jigger, pointed to a larger glass on the backbar. "Make it out of those doubles or triples so I can taste the stuff, will you?" he grunted.

The bartender bared discolored teeth in what passed for a smile, selected a larger glass, tilted the bottle over it. "Ain't seen you around here before." There was a trace of a lisp in his simpering tone. "Looking for somebody special?"

Liddell picked up his glass, turned his back to the bar, glanced out over the tables.

"If it's not somebody special, there are a lot of nice—" the bartender persisted.

Liddell swung around to him. "Look, friend. I'm looking for somebody special. You're not it. Leave the bottle here. I'll call you when I need you."

The fat man's eyes receded behind their discolored pouches; a muscle flicked in the side of his throat. The fat, wet lips puffed in and out in indignation, leaving a little bubble between them. For a moment Liddell thought he was going to retort, but instead the man turned and flounced to the far end of the bar where the two Marines and the gowned man were getting loud and gay.

Liddell leaned on the bar, twitched his nose at the faint smell of incense in the air. He turned at a touch on his elbow. It was a thin young man with long, wavy black hair. His eyebrows were penciled to a thin hairline, there was a mustache to match on his upper lip. He was wearing a powder-blue suit and a flaming-red tie.

"Are you Liddell?" The swish in his voice was almost undetectable.

Liddell nodded, looked the boy over insolently. He looked like a particularly prosperous chorus boy except for the slight bulge under the handkerchief in his breast pocket. Otherwise the suit was faultlessly tailored, fitted snugly.

"Will you come with me?" he requested, turned on his heel, led the way through the welter of tables.

Liddell waited until his guide was halfway across the room, followed slowly. At the far end of the room a disguised stairway led to an upper floor. At the top of the stairs, there was a long hallway with a row of closed doors, an overpowering smell of perfume and cologne and the muffled sounds of revelry.

Liddell caught the young man by the arm. "Let's get something straight, buster," he told him. "I'm here on business."

An ugly red flush mottled the man's dark skin. He shook his arm free with an effeminate gesture. "Don't flatter yourself, Liddell. I'm just doing this as a favor for my friend Hunt." He turned away angrily, led the way down the hall to a closed door, knocked. "It's I, dear," he simpered to the closed door.

After a moment, a key scraped in the lock, the door opened a crack, then as though the viewer was satisfied, the door swung open wide. Tim, Brin's bodyguard, glared at Liddell. "Come in, peeper." Inside the room, Hunt Brin sat, taking short, nervous puffs out of a cigarette.

Liddell stepped into the room, nodded to Brin. The door swung shut behind him. "Get your tough boy out of here, Brin, or we don't talk," Liddell told him.

Tim's voice grated in his ear from behind. "You're in no spot to be handing out orders, Liddell. Besides, you and me have a little deal to finish up."

Liddell turned negligently. "We can have our dance some other time, junior. Right now, we're busy."

The bodyguard's lips flattened back over his teeth. "You asked for it, peeper!" His hand flashed to his pocket, came up with a switch knife. "We'll see how tough you really are."

"Cut it out, Tim," Hunt Brin's voice lashed out like a whip. "Cut it out or I'll let you have it."

The rage drained out of Tim's face, to be replaced by shock. Liddell turned to see a .38 in Brin's hand aimed at the bodyguard's middle.

"You crazy, Hunt? This is Tim. You wouldn't."

The gun muzzle never wavered. "I told you this guy can't be hurt. He's got to get me off the hook on the murder rap. If it's going to be you or me, Tim, don't start reading any continued stories." He waved the gun contemptuously. "You better wait outside."

Tim hesitated, hopscotched his eyes from Brin to Liddell and back. "Okay, Hunt. You're the boss." He returned the knife to a jacket pocket, opened the door, stalked out.

"You can turn around now, Liddell," Brin growled. He still held the gun. "You can push your luck too far. Some day you're going to push it too far."

"That'll be tough on you, chum," Liddell grinned. "Tougher than on me."

Brin's face went white under its tan. He made a half-hearted attempt at the lazy smile, gave it up as a bad job. "You've got aces back to back, probably," he conceded. "But take the advice of a professional gambler. Don't ever push too hard on one pair."

Liddell nodded, found an armchair, dropped into it. "I've done a little gambling in my time, too. I know a few rules of my own. Such as never bluff when there's no limit on table stakes."

Brin stared hard for a moment, then shrugged. "Okay, so you're calling my bluff. Let's hear your proposition."

"I want Goldy. I want about forty-five minutes with her. You finger her for me, and I'll clear you on the Lunfaro killing."

Brin laid the .38 on the arm of his chair, found a pack of cigarettes in his jacket pocket. There was a thin film of perspiration on his upper lip. "Suppose you walk in on Goldy and can't walk out?"

Liddell shrugged. "I wasn't figuring on living forever."

"How about me?"

"You're out of luck," Liddell grunted. "Your part of the deal is to fix it so's I see Goldy without having any trouble."

Brin wiped the perspiration off his lip, stuck a cigarette in his mouth, touched the glow of a lighter to it. "You've got me in a box," he growled. "If it ever gets out that I fingered her for you, my life won't be worth a dime."

Liddell grinned. "It's not worth a tenth of that now. Every cop in town is looking for you, and when they get you, you're due to be the queen of the dance hall at Sing Sing."

The cigarette in Brin's mouth wavered crazily. "What makes you think they'll believe you about the fingerprints?"

"Because if you go through with your end of the deal, I'll have the real killer, all signed, sealed, and delivered," Liddell told him. "Well?"

"All right. I have no choice." Brin moistened his lower lip with the tip of his tongue. "She's hiding out in Chinatown. Ben Cerla's taking care of her." His hand shook noticeably as he returned his cigarette to his lips. "It's an old opium den behind the Fan Tan setup. She went under cover because she spotted you at the Breen the other night, knew you'd recognized her."

Liddell nodded. "Go on."

Brin shook his head stubbornly. "That's all. I fingered Goldy for you. That was our deal."

"Who's bossing this deal, Brin? Who's behind the big racket?"

The color drained out of the blond man's face. He wiped his lips with the back of his hand, shook his head. "I'm not doing any more talking. We had a deal, and—" A buzzer clicked somewhere. Brin reached for the phone at his elbow, listened for a moment. He nodded jerkily. "I been trying to reach you. All right, I'll be right out." He hung the receiver up. "I'll be right back, Liddell. Wait here."

Liddell nodded, leaned back, lit a cigarette. He was on his second cigarette when the hunch that something had gone wrong became a certainty. He stepped to the door, listened. There was no sound from the hall. He opened the door a crack, peered out. The hallway was deserted. He pulled the snub-nosed .38 from his jacket pocket, wished fervently he had his .45.

There was nobody in the hallway when he stepped out. From behind closed doors he could still detect the high, shrill note of revelry. Softly he closed the door behind him, started down the hallway.

He caught a flash of motion in the corner of his eye, saw a door on the opposite side of the corridor open slowly. Liddell crouched back against the wall, waited.

Tim, Brin's bodyguard, stepped through the open door, raised his arm. Liddell caught a flash of metal in the subdued light, there was a whiz, then a thud as the knife bit into the wall near his head.

Liddell squeezed the trigger twice. The .38 barked like a cannon in the confined space. Tim straightened up as though he were reaching for something. As he stretched upward to his full height, Liddell fired again. The other man seemed to deflate, dropped as though his knees had been cut from under him. The surprised expression was still on his face as he hit the floor. He didn't move.

There was a moment of complete silence, then a moment of pandemonium. High-pitched voices screamed, heavier voices cursed, doors opened and slammed. There was still no sign of Hunt Brin.

Liddell walked over to where Tim lay, looked into the room beyond. It was empty. Outside there was a pounding of footsteps on the stairs as the occupants of the bar below rushed up to investigate. Liddell stepped across Tim's body, dragged it into the room, bolted the door after him.

He tried the window, found it slid up easily, leaned out. There was an easy drop to the littered alleyway below, another open window a few feet away. He was about to drop to the alley when through the open window he saw a familiar figure. Hunt Brin was sitting in a chair with his back to the window. Liddell swung his leg over the sill, reached for the other window. He swung himself across the opening, landed in the other room.

Hunt Brin sat there alone in the room, watching the door. Liddell walked up behind him, caught him by the shoulder.

"Wouldn't be waiting for me to stick my face in that door, would you, Brin?" he asked.

The man in the chair tilted forward, hit the floor face first. He lay there unmoving. Liddell was at his side, turned him over on his back. The old lazy smile was back on Brin's face, but it looked permanent. His eyes were half open, his throat had been cut almost from ear to ear. It didn't take an expert to detect that Hunt Brin could be depended upon to spill no more of the gang's secrets.

Outside in the hall were sounds of a growing tumult.

There was a knock on the door. "Everything all right in there?" a voice demanded.

Liddell pretended indignation. "Of course. Leave us alone."

There was silence from the hall. Then another knock across the hall, the same question. The room in which Tim's body lay would be the next, Liddell knew. He rushed back to the window, slid over the sill, dropped to the alleyway. It brought him right out on Waverly Place where the neon stained the sidewalk a deep red, almost the same color as Brin's blood had stained the floor in his death chamber. There was no sign that the police had been called, or would be called to investigate the shooting.

Liddell headed for Seventh Avenue and a cab.

CHAPTER FOURTEEN

JOHNNY LIDDELL WALKED SLOWLY down a side street in Chinatown that had so far shucked the Occidental atmosphere that he might well have been walking down a street in the native quarter of Shanghai. Here were the stores that did not cater to tourists, where Chinese sold to Chinese, where the merchandise was too exotic and sometimes too strong for the Occidental palate, where nationally advertised patent medicines had made way on the shelves of apothecaries to potions compiled of portions of reptiles and rodents.

Here the tourist never penetrated and no other white man was to be seen on the street. The elderly Chinese shuffled by, their wrinkled faces placid, their pace un-hurried. The younger Chinese seemed self-conscious and vaguely uncomfortable in their western clothes as they too, adopted the traditional shuffle of the East.

After walking several blocks, Johnny Liddell found what he was looking for. An elderly Chinese lounged against a doorway, his face calm, his eyes at rest. He regarded Liddell incuriously as the private detective walked up to him.

"Where's the game going on, pop?" Liddell asked.

There was no change of expression in the wrinkled face. The old man shrugged his shoulders, shook his head, looked away.

Liddell eased a roll of bills from his pocket, slid out a twenty. "Fan Tan. I want to play," He told the old man.

"There won't be any trouble. I just want to know where they're playing."

The old man looked from Liddell to the twenty and back, grinned a toothless grin. "Who know?" he chattered.

"You know," Liddell told him. He added another twenty, let the old man see. "You get self pretty girl, plenty dreams." He held out the bills. "No trouble."

The Chinese shook his head. "Me no know." He shrugged his shoulders expressively, looked past Liddell as though he had lost interest.

Liddell growled under his breath, decided on a last-ditch try, fished into his wallet, came up with the chit signed by Eddie Sung. "Me good friend Eddie Sung in Frisco." Liddell pushed the card under the old man's nose.

The old man grunted, looked away.

Liddell considered the advisability of pushing his way past the old man, realized the game might be blocks away through a maze of passageways, decided against it as futile, turned on his heel, walked on. The old man gave no sign that he had noticed Liddell had left.

That the old man was an outside watcher for the game, Liddell was convinced. That meant that the game was probably running some place within a five-block radius, he estimated, decided to check the restaurants in that area for the telltale "bank" table.

He wandered in and out of three restaurants before he found the one he was seeking. At a large table, in the center of the floor, a group of round-faced, uncommunicative Chinese were huddled around a huge pot in the center of the table.

They would dip into the pot of steaming food, slop it onto their plate, hold the plate close to their mouths, shovel it in. No one at the table talked to anyone else. As soon as one diner was finished he would get up, leave without paying, his place immediately filled by another equally hungry, equally uncommunicative Chinese.

Liddell walked over to the cashier, dropped a five, called for a pack of cigarettes. The girl working the cash register had the finely boned features of a wellborn Chinese, over which had been superimposed the cosmetics, the sleek coiffure, and the assurance of a western woman. She slid the cigarettes across the counter, dropped four ones and some change beside them.

"Never mind the change," Liddell told her.

The girl looked up through long lashes, studied him quizzically.

"Seeing the sights," Liddell explained. He indicated the round table of men. "They must be from the Fan Tan game I've been hearing about."

The girl looked past him to the table, nodded. "Perhaps."

Liddell broke open the pack of cigarettes. "Well, you're certainly not running a mission here. Nobody at that table seems to pay for anything."

"We are paid for everything served at that table," the girl told him. "Some of those men may be Fan Tan players, but most are unfortunates. Their food is paid for."

Liddell hung the cigarette from the corner of his mouth. "Home relief?" He took a wooden match from the container on the counter, scratched it, applied it to the cigarette.

"Our less fortunate citizens need not look to outsiders for aid," the girl told him coldly. "There are no Chinese beggars. The Fan-Tan banks see to it that all unfortunates may eat. It is tradition."

Liddell looked impressed. "That's wonderful. I'd like to see this Fan-Tan being played. Know where the game's going on?"

The girl shrugged. "I do not know. But I do not think you will be able to see the game."

"Why not?"

"It is for Chinese only. Americans are not welcome in the gaming room." She pushed the bills and change to him. "It is foolish and a waste of time trying to bribe somebody to get you in. It would be impossible, maybe very dangerous."

Liddell shrugged. "It was just an idea." He pushed the money back across the counter. "Consider that a contribution toward feeding the unfortunate."

For the first time the girl smiled. "Thank you." She picked up the bills, folded them, put them in the slot of a large jar marked with Chinese figures. "In here it will be used to relieve the suffering of unfortunates in China. Over here, we need no help in taking care of our own." She turned, busied herself with an open ledger.

In the street again, Liddell debated the advisability of waiting for one of the men at the Fan Tan table to leave, then following him, decided against it. He smoked his cigarette irritably, wondering how he was going to crash the gate, and get to Goldy and Cerla in the old opium den beyond the game room.

He was so deep in thought, he failed to notice the young Chinese who sidled up to him. "Liddell?" he asked huskily.

Liddell startled, looked at the speaker. He was taller than the average Chinese dressed in western clothes had the same expressionless countenance as the others.

"I'm Liddell. Why?"

"You have been trying to reach an important member of our community. He has returned earlier than was expected and is anxious to have conversation with you," the Chinese told him.

"Kaiming?"

The other man nodded. "He is now available. If you have no more pressing business, he would like you to drop by his office."

Liddell tossed his cigarette toward the curb. "Wonderful. He may be just the man I want to see."

Johnny Liddell walked through the unmarked door next to the Chinese grocery, into the dusty vestibule. He walked up the rickety stairs to the paint-peeled door above, stepped through, stopped in front of the huge one-way glass door. After a moment, the familiar click of the circuit breaker broke the silence, and the door swung open. Jimmy Kaiming was waiting on the other side.

"We seem to have been missing each other all day," Kaiming greeted him as Liddell entered. He waved the detective to a chair. "Was there something important you wanted me for?"

Liddell sank into the chair, shook his head. "Returning your call. By the way, how did you know where to find me?"

Kaiming shrugged, smiled. "You have been making inquiries in Chinatown. Naturally, that comes to my ears."

Liddell nodded glumly. "If I had been able to reach you, I wouldn't have had to go through all the motions."

"You sound tired. Perhaps if we had some refreshments?" Kaiming clapped his hands and the doll-like little Chinese girl stepped into the room. "Some bourbon and water, Fah Soo," Kaiming told her.

Fah Soo bowed her head slightly, smiled at Liddell, stepped back through the concealed door in the paneling.

"Now, perhaps you would like to tell me what you have been trying to find in Chinatown?" Kaiming suggested. He found a cigarette, stuck it in his holder, tilted it from the corner of his mouth.

"I've been trying to find where the Fan-Tan game is going on," Liddell growled. "Do you know?"

Kaiming frowned slightly, snapped his lighter into flame, touched it to the end of his cigarette. "I know. But I do not think it would be wise for you to attempt to crash it."

"Couldn't you okay me through?"

The tong leader shook his head. "Unfortunately, no. Let me explain." He blew a stream of smoke at the ceiling, seemed to be picking his words carefully. "You know something of tong organization? You may know that today our tong has not the power here in the East that it enjoys in the West where our mutual friend Eddie Sung is all-powerful."

"I didn't know."

Kaiming nodded. "Not very long ago, the tongs here waged a bloody and futile war. We were not victorious. We were almost destroyed. Had it not been for the help of our other branches in other cities, our tong would have been smashed." He tapped the end of the cigarette holder against his teeth. "The victors have taken the spoils. They run the Fan Tan, they have the choice locations for their activities."

Liddell rubbed at the side of his jaw. "Top dog takes over the juiciest territory, leaves the crumbs for the others, eh?"

"It has been that way until now," Kaiming told him softly. "It will not always be that way."

"I wouldn't want you to start a tong war just to get me into a Fan Tan setup," Liddell growled.

Kaiming went through the motions of a smile. "I gather from your eagerness to get into this Fan Tan game that something has happened?"

Liddell nodded. "Plenty." He waited while the girl returned, placed a bottle, some glasses, and ice on the table, glided back through the door. "I think I've found who's behind the whole setup."

"Wonderful. Who is it?"

"Cerla. And a woman named Goldy. A hustler."

Kaiming considered it, let twin streams of smoke dribble from his nostrils. "You have enough to go to the police?"

Liddell shook his head. "Not until I've been able to talk to Goldy. That's why I want so badly to find where the Fan-Tan game is. Cerla's hiding her out in an old den just beyond the game room."

"You're sure of this?"

"Sure enough. The guy that told me is dead."

Kaiming nodded. "I read of that. His name was Lunfaro, was it not?"

"That was yesterday." Liddell grinned humorlessly. "Tonight it was his boss. Cerla's partner. A guy named Hunt Brin."

The cigarette holder sagged in the corner of Kaiming's mouth. "You killed him?"

Liddell reached over, spilled some ice and bourbon into a glass. "His bodyguard cut Brin's throat." He added some water to the bourbon. "I had to kill the bodyguard in self-defense."

"I see." There was no change in Kaiming's expression. His dark eyes studied Liddell, then dropped as the private detective returned his gaze. "And all this killing is connected with the case on which you are working?"

"They're all part of the same pattern."

Kaiming sighed. "It seems difficult for me to see how the death of a friendless and unknown Chinese could be connected with the deaths of a society figure and a hired gunman."

"You'll have to take my word for it."

Kaiming shrugged. "As you say." He adjusted the cigarette holder in the corner of his mouth. "But suppose this man who told you where the woman is hiding lied to you?"

Liddell sipped at his glass, shook his head. "He wouldn't. I had too much of a lever on him."

"Brin?" Kaiming shrugged. "According to the newspapers he was wanted by the police for the murder of Lunfaro. What has such a man to lose?"

"Nothing. But he had plenty to gain."

"Such as?"

Liddell drained the glass, set it down. "I could have cleared him of that murder charge. Brin didn't kill Lunfaro."

Kaiming raised his eyebrows. "But the gun. It had his fingerprints on it. The police identified him as the killer."

"He was framed. I was the only one who could prove it, so we made a deal. He told me where Goldy was, I was going to square him with the cops."

The Chinese regarded Liddell unblinkingly. He continued to puff lightly on his cigarette. "Now you wish to see this Goldy? Why not just give what you know to the police?"

"I don't have enough. If I can talk to her just for a few minutes I will have." He leaned forward. "You've got to get me in where I can get at her."

Kaiming removed the holder from between his teeth, scowled at it. "No white men are permitted to engage in Fan Tan, even to watch. It is the rule." He removed the cigarette from the holder, crushed it in a black onyx ashtray.

"There must be some way," Liddell persisted.

The Chinese pursed his lips, stared at the crushed cigarette. "There is a way," he admitted. His eyes rolled up, regarded Liddell through their lashes. "It is, you understand, very dangerous. The tong controlling the game do not look with pleasure upon an invasion of their territory."

"Tell me where it is. I'll take my chances."

Kaiming sighed deeply. "You understand that you will be going into forbidden territory—that I cannot guarantee your safety or even offer any assistance once you enter that territory?"

"Let me do the worrying. You just get me past the watchers."

"That will present no difficulty," Kaiming muttered. "I can even arrange for your guidance through the passages to where the game is played and to the den beyond where you say this woman is hidden. I cannot guarantee you a safe return. You still wish to make this trip?"

"The sooner the better. As soon as Goldy hears of Brin's death, she and Cerla may change their hiding place. Then I've got to start all over."

Kaiming shrugged. "If you insist on this foolhardy expedition, I can only do my best to help. I will arrange for you to by-pass the guards. You will be guided to where the game is in operation. From there on, I can only hope for your safety."

Liddell stood up. "What do I do?"

Kaiming consulted his watch. "You will go to the Hat Soy Yen Trading Company on Pell Street. There will be a person behind the counter who will expect you." He stood up, extended his hand. "I can only wish you luck."

There was a sharp buzz from the door. Jimmy Kaiming walked to the door, looked through, signaled for Liddell.

Outside the door stood Inspector Herlehy. He shuffled his feet impatiently, stared at the opaque side of the door, unaware that he was being watched from within. After a moment, he stabbed at the bell at the side of the door and the buzz in the room was repeated.

"You wish to see the police?" Kaiming asked.

"Not right now." Liddell shook his head.

Kaiming nodded, clapped his hands. Fah Soo emerged from the hidden door. "You will let Mr. Liddell out the back entrance," Kaiming ordered.

Fah Soo bowed, stepped aside for Liddell to precede her. He walked through the hidden door, which slid shut behind him. He was in a living room exquisitely furnished with priceless evidence of Oriental artistry. Minute bits of ivory and jade had been carved with such attention to detail that a figure the size of a fingernail was perfect even to the skin texture of the carved elephant. The furniture was massive, carved black teakwood, and the walls were draped with brightly tinted silks.

Liddell followed the girl through four other rooms to a huge, barred door. "This will lead you through to another square," she told him. "You will descend the stairs, arrive safely on the street. You will not be bothered." She lifted the heavy cross bar on the door, opened it noiselessly.

Liddell walked through, found himself facing an old, paint-peeled door similar to the one he had entered through. He opened the door, descended a flight of rickety steps, passed through into the cool, fresh air of the street a block removed from the grocery store through which he had entered Kaiming's office.

CHAPTER FIFTEEN

A THIN, STOOP-SHOULDERED young Chinese looked up as Johnny Liddell entered the office of the Hat Soy Yen Trading Company. He peered at him through thick-lensed glasses. "You wish to see somebody, sir?" His voice was sing-songy, shrill.

"I'm a friend of Jimmy Kaiming. He told me somebody would be expecting me here."

The Chinese nodded his head several times. "I have been expecting you, sir." He signaled for an elderly Chinese to take his place at the books he had been poring over. "I have had my instructions. You will please come with me."

He led the way to the street, passed a group of stores, stopped in front of one store whose windows were piled high with a miscellany of junk. Inside, a man was sitting at a white enameled kitchen table that served as a desk, painting Chinese characters on an orange sheet of paper. He used a camel's hairbrush held perpendicularly between thumb and forefinger. He glanced up as they entered, listened while the spectacled man told him something in liquid Cantonese, dropped his eyes, went back to his painting.

There was a curtained recess in the back of the store. The young Chinese motioned for Liddell to follow him, led the way through into a small room beyond. At the far wall, he fingered the molding, found a button that had been cleverly disguised in the wood. A door slid noiselessly open. They stepped into the narrow, dim passageway beyond, closed the door behind them.

Liddell stayed close to the Chinese as he led the way through the damp passage, came to a room where a group of Chinese were playing Chinese dominoes. They didn't even look up as Liddell and the guide walked through and entered another passageway. After a few minutes, they came into another room, evidently a catchall for the shops above it. Odds and ends were stored in confusion. Old furniture and crates of merchandise were piled to the ceiling.

The Chinese picked his way through the crates, slid open another wall panel, waited for Liddell to follow before he slid the panel shut behind them. They were in complete darkness now except for the pale glow of a flashlight the Chinese brought from his jacket pocket. Liddell followed him down a flight of rough-hewn steps into another passageway that smelled of dampness. After a few steps they went down another flight of steps, evidently passing under some road above, Liddell realized. A hundred feet farther they started to climb a flight of steps to what appeared to be a blank wall.

"Beyond this I may not go," the guide told him. "To be found in the forbidden territory of a rival tong might mean death for me."

Liddell nodded. "What do I do?"

"I will arrange for you to enter the passage to the gaming room. Beyond that is a passageway that leads to the opium parlor you seek."

"Okay. That's all I want," Liddell told him. "Thanks."

"I hope you will continue to be thankful," the Chinese muttered. He ran his fingers over the edge of the wall. A whole section seemed to swing out of position, operated by an electrical mechanism that whirred as the door opened. "You will follow this passage for a hundred yards. There you will see the Fan Tan. The passageway lies on the far side of the tables. Good-by, sir."

He turned on his heel, started back the way they had come. Liddell watched the glow of the flashlight receding until the dip in the passageway hid it from sight. Then he stepped through the door, heard the whirr of the mechanism as it slid into place behind him, started up the passageway.

Soon he became aware of a low hum of conversation. A large room loomed at a bend in the passageway. He walked in.

There were two large tables, each presided over by a stickman armed with a bamboo stick and pot cover. Each corner of the table was marked in bright paint with a number from one to four. As the players would heap stacks of bills on a selected corner, the stickman would reach into a pot of beans at his elbow, spill a handful of the beans on the table, cover as many as he could with the pot cover. Then, using the bamboo stick, he cleared the surplus from the table. As soon as the uncovered beans were cleared off, he lifted the pot cover, counted the beans under it four at a time. The players on the corner represented by the number left were paid off at the rate of three to one.

The absorption of the players in the game was so intense that not an eye rose as Liddell walked in. He watched the play for a few minutes; then, spotting the entrance to the other passageway on the far side of the room, he elbowed his way through the players, headed for it.

He paused for a moment at the entrance to the other passageway. There was no light visible. He plunged in, felt his way along the damp wall. About a hundred feet from the Fan-Tan room he started to climb sharply. A sickly-sweet scent started to assail his nostrils and he fought an impulse to sneeze. Ahead he could see some evidence of light. He started toward the source of the light slowly, brought the .38 from his pocket, held it at readiness.

The only warning was the scraping of a heel behind him. He tried to spin in to meet whatever was coming, failed to duck the blackjack. It caught him a flush blow on the head, knocked him to his knees. He was dimly aware that as he fell his gun slipped out of his hand, skidded into the darkness of the corridor. He reached out, tried to grapple with his assailant, caught a pair of legs—sheathed in a skirt.

The sap landed twice more, and he knew the power had flowed out of his hands. There was a series of flashing multicolored lights that merged into a crazy, blinding pattern.

The only sound was the deafening sobs of someone breathing, the rushing of the blood in his ears.

The bright colors ebbed and flowed before his eyes until a flood of darkness came in to blot them out. Liddell wasn't even aware of the two men who grabbed him roughly by the shoulders, dragged him through the passageway into the room ahead.

It was the strident quality of the voices that persuaded Liddell that he was still alive. Each time the speaker emphasized a point, it drove red-hot irons through his skull. He had difficulty remembering where he was, or what had happened, but bits began to come back to him.

He tried to move his arms, found them bound behind his back. His legs had been similarly treated. From the stuffiness of his quarters, he guessed that he had been dumped into a closet some place.

Outside, the strident tones continued to pierce the thin closet wall and send spears of pain to the back of Liddell's eyes. He was aware that one of the voices had a familiar tone, but it took moments of attempted concentration before he knew why it sounded familiar. It was the nasal, flat voice of Goldy, the woman he had come seeking. He strained his ears to hear what she was saying.

"I tell you with Hunt dead we've got to handle this ourselves, Ben," she insisted. "We've got to get it through. Things are getting hot, and I want to get out. But I want to get mine before I do."

The other voice seemed to protest, but Goldy shouted him down.

"They'll pay plenty for this stuff, I tell you. Brin took a lot of chances getting these plans for them. They'll pay plenty. And there's only a two-way cut now." She continued to pour the persuasion on heavily. "We can't wait any longer. The feds will find out this stuff is missing from the files and the heat will really shrivel us."

The other voice continued to protest, but less vigor ously now. Liddell couldn't make out the words, but the tone of surrender was apparent.

"I knew you'd be smart," Goldy exulted. "You set it up for us to get out of here. You can handle the shortwave as well as Hunt ever could. We can get this stuff over to them tonight, then hole up until the payoff."

Liddell struggled with his bonds, felt one of the ropes slip, started to work on it in earnest. Here was an angle even the Treasury Department didn't have, the sale of military secrets, the existence of an unsuspected shortwave contact with a foreign power. The ransom setup had overflowed into espionage!

Inside the room there were sounds of the two making ready to leave. When footsteps approached where he was sprawled out, he slumped back, feigned unconsciousness.

The closet door opened, a flash of light almost blinded Liddell as it flowed from the room into the closet's dark recesses. He could smell the cheap perfume as Goldy leaned over him, peered at him closely. Then the door swung shut, cutting off the light. But it was not shut closely enough to shut off sound.

"You know the way to the sending-station alone, don't you, Ben?" Goldy asked.

Cerla's voice was querulous. "Of course I know where it is. It was my idea to use a boat so's they couldn't trace where it was."

Goldy grunted. "Okay, so you're a Big Brain. So it was your idea to use the *Sea Nymph*. All I got to say is it's good the idea worked out. You only get one wrong guess in this racket." There was the sound of a chair scraping back. "Let's go."

Liddell waited until he heard the sound of a door closing in the outer chamber, then started to work on his bonds. The loop around his right wrist started to slip, made a slack that gave him something to work with.

The perspiration beaded his forehead, rolled down into his eyes, blinding him. He swore under his breath as the rope cut into his flesh, worked all the harder. After what seemed hours, the loop slipped over his wrist, freeing his hand. It was a matter of minutes to free his other hand and his feet.

He lay quietly for a minute, breathing heavily from the exertion. He could feel the blood rushing back into his cramped arms and legs. When he felt he could stand, he pulled himself painfully to his feet, steadied himself against the door.

Cautiously he pushed the door open, found himself in a large, empty room with built-in bunks lining the three walls. The plaster hung damply from the ceiling in chunks, the bunks were covered with rags bunched at the feet of them.

He made his way to a washbasin in the corner, stared at himself in the cracked mirror that hung crazily askew above it. His face was a mass of dried blood where a gash in his scalp had bled freely. He doused the cold water into his face, washed away the blood, dried himself with a handkerchief. He pushed his hair back out of his face, flattened it gently with water. After a moment, he looked almost human.

The cold water helped clear his head as well. He looked around for a way out of the room that would not necessitate returning the way he had come. There was a door that led to what looked like a small hall. He walked over, opened the door a crack, listened. There was no sound. He swung the door all the way open, stuck his head through. He found himself at the head of a rickety flight of stairs. The house seemed vacant.

Liddell stepped to the top of the stairs, started down. At the landing, he could see the room below. It looked like the lobby of a small hotel of sorts. The room was partitioned off with discolored plywood into an office in which there was a desk, a telephone on the wall, a rack of old-fashioned keys. It was presided over by a thin, undersized Chinese clerk.

Liddell decided to take his chances on making it. With no one in the lobby but the clerk, he estimated his chances as good. He continued down the steps.

When he reached the bottom, the clerk looked up, stared at him impersonally, nodded, went back to his study of the vertical columns of the Chinese newspaper spread out on the desk before him.

Liddell walked past the desk, made the street. Outside, he recognized landmarks identifying the place as blocks from the store where he had first entered the Fan-Tan maze. He headed up the street for the Bowery and a telephone.

As Johnny Liddell looked up from his third cup of coffee, Muggsy Kiely slid into the seat beside him. She stared at the discolored gash just under the hairline, whistled soundlessly.

"You're a detective who really uses his head, aren't you? What happened?"

"I got too close to Goldy, and she let me have it. With a sap." He investigated the top of his head gingerly. "And don't think that baby doesn't know how to use one."

"You got close to her?"

Liddell nodded, swore as the pains shot through his head. "I was sneaking up on her. She must have heard me, because she waited until I got close enough, then she lowered the boom."

"You're sure it was Goldy?"

"Positive. When I started to go out, I grabbed for whoever it was. I got a handful of skirt." He finished his coffee, signaled the waitress to bring two more cups. "When I came to, she was sitting in the room with Ben Cerla."

"Too bad you couldn't hold onto her."

Liddell grimaced. "Too bad my skull isn't steel-plated. Did you get what I wanted?"

"Maybe."

"What do you mean, maybe? I told you it was rush. Did you get it?"

Muggsy waited until the waitress had placed the coffee in front of them and retired beyond earshot. "Where do I fit in this deal, Johnny?" she wanted to know.

"We've been through all that. I'll call you and give you the stuff the minute it happens."

Muggsy shook her head. "That *was* the deal. This story's getting bigger all the time, I want to be in on the finish. Firsthand-observer stuff."

"Nothing doing. These people are killers. I tell you they've got nothing to lose. They're a gang of spies and they're in a corner."

"Either I go, Johnny, or I don't give you the location of the *Sea Nymph*."

Liddell muttered fervently under his breath. "Okay, play cute. Act like a dame. I'll get it some place else."

Muggsy sampled her coffee, added more sugar. "Go ahead. By the time you get it, they'll be gone. If you could have gotten it, you wouldn't have called me," she added sweetly.

Liddell shook his head. "No deal."

Muggsy shrugged. "Okay. But if I were you, I'd be sensible and let me come along."

Liddell stole a look at his watch, groaned. "Okay, you win. But don't forget. You asked for it. Now, give. Where's the *Sea Nymph*?"

"Manhasset Bay harbor. Out on the Island. She's a big power cruiser." Muggsy fumbled through her bag, came up with a piece of copy paper bearing a set of scribbled notations. "Registered in the name of Huntington Brin." She looked up. "Sound familiar?"

"That does it. That ties this up in a nice fancy package." He dumped a handful of silver on the table, started to get up.

"What are you going to do, Johnny?"

"What do you think I'm going to do? I'm going out to the boat and try evening the score with that antediluvian Magdalene and that rat Cerla. Then I'm calling in the T-boys and dumping the whole mess into their laps, all wrapped up in pretty pink paper."

"I think you'd better wait and call them in first."

"You crazy? This is personal now. They've been playing Ravel's 'Bolero' on my skull for too long." He peered suspiciously at Muggsy. "What do you mean wait?"

Muggsy chewed on the end of a fingernail, raised penitent eyes. "I called Herlehy and told him we'd meet him here."

Liddell's jaw dropped. *"Why?"*

Muggsy caught his arm. "Look, Johnny, be reasonable. This thing is too big to do alone. You'll end up in the electric chair or the bottom of the harbor."

"What do you mean electric chair? They've got nothing on me."

"They think they have, Johnny. They're sure you killed Lunfaro, framed Brin for it, and then killed him. You knew Brin and his bodyguard were dead?"

Liddell nodded.

"You, Johnny?" Muggsy asked.

"I got the bodyguard. He came at me with a shiv. I don't know who killed Brin, but I know why. He was beginning to spill too much to me."

"Just the same, Johnny, you can't stick your neck out any more. You've done all you can. Let the feds move in and clean up."

Liddell pulled his arm away angrily. "Why should I? I did all the work and took all the risks. This is my baby and I'm staying out front until I wrap it up. When Herlehy gets here, you can tell him—"

"Tell him yourself, Johnny," Muggsy said.

Outside a squad car, siren screaming, skidded to a stop, and Herlehy stepped out.

The inspector walked in, ignored the curious stares of the other diners, nodded to Muggsy, scowled at Liddell. "So I finally caught up with you, eh? I knew I was right. I should have locked you up and thrown the key away when I had you in on that Lunfaro job. A guy like you plays hell with mortality tables. What's going on?"

Liddell took a fast look at the time, decided to play it straight. He dropped into a chair, brought Herlehy up to date on what had happened since he put the pressure on Brin at Marty's Place. Herlehy almost forgot to chew his ever-present gum during the telling. As soon as Liddell had explained the existence of the shortwave set aboard the *Sea Nymph*, the inspector jumped to his feet.

"What are you sitting around here for? We gotta get going."

"How about the harbor police, inspector?" Muggsy suggested. "Can't we get them to move in on the *Sea Nymph?*"

"Not out in Manhasset Bay, Muggsy," Herlehy grunted. "We can get there faster." He led the way back to the squad car. "Manhasset Bay, Mickey," he told the driver, "and really let her roar. Cut your siren before we get into Manhasset. This is a surprise party, and we're not invited."

CHAPTER SIXTEEN

THE *Sea Nymph* was a long, sleek black shadow moored to the dock at Manhasset Bay. The tall, slim snout of an antenna poked upward toward the first streaks of dawn in the sky.

Johnny Liddell, Inspector Herlehy, and Muggsy Kiely left the squad car a block from the mooring, approached on foot. They melted into the shadows of a building a stone's throw from where a gangplank connected the ship and the dock.

"You'd better stay here, Muggs, until we know what we're likely to run into," Johnny Liddell whispered.

"Nothing doing." Muggsy shook her head vigorously. "We got a deal. I come aboard with you."

"Liddell's right," Herlehy put in. "We'd better try it alone first, Muggsy. You'll be in at the finish," he promised.

Muggsy started to argue, decided she was outnumbered. "Okay. But I'm coming aboard just the same. I'll wait here fifteen minutes," she conceded. "Then I'm coming up."

"Okay, okay." Liddell nodded. "Let's go, inspector."

They hugged the shadow of the building as far as it would cover them. Then, dodging from dark spot to dark spot, they halted behind a large case at the foot of the gangplank.

"This is going to be the tough part, if they've got a lookout posted," Liddell whispered. "I'll go first. You've got the gun. Cover me."

Herlehy nodded, fumbled under his jacket, came up with his service revolver. "Okay, Liddell. Good luck."

Liddell nodded, peered from behind the huge packing case at the dock's edge up at the ship. There was no sign of a lookout. As quietly as he could, he made his way to the gangplank, crept up it, made the deck of the ship with no trouble. He crouched in the shadow of the superstructure, watched breathlessly as Herlehy followed.

"No sign of life?" Herlehy panted.

Liddell caught his sleeve, pointed to the bow. In the darkness, a pinpoint of light glowed brightly, then died away. "He's been there all the time," Liddell whispered, "but I guess he hasn't been expecting any company. I'll take him."

Herlehy nodded, melted back into the shadows.

Liddell crept forward on all fours until he could make out the shadowy form of the man smoking a cigarette. The cigarette glowed and died as the man took a last deep drag on it, then it cut a wide arc in the darkness as he flipped it out into the water. Liddell flattened back against the side of the cabin as the man got up, started toward him. He was small, narrow-shouldered, walked with a peculiarly shuffling motion. Chinese!

He saw Johnny Liddell almost at the moment Liddell sprang. He opened his mouth to shout a warning or call for help, but nothing but a strangled grunt came out when Liddell drove the tips of his extended fingers into the Chinese's Adam's apple.

Liddell brushed aside the arm that was on its way to the guard's holster, hit him a staggering blow that dropped him to the deck with a thud.

There was a scraping noise behind him. Liddell swung, recognized Herlehy.

"Get him?" Herlehy whispered.

Liddell nodded, bent down alongside the unconscious man, squinted at him, grunted.

"Know him?" Herlehy asked.

"Cerla's bodyguard. Saw him at the Chinese Heaven." He pulled the gun from the Chinese's holster, jammed it into his jacket pocket, motioned for Herlehy to help him. They dragged the Chinese to the bow of the boat, handcuffed his hands around the railing. "Just in case he gets wanderlust," Liddell grunted. He pulled the handkerchief from the man's breast pocket, jammed it between his teeth. "In case he gets lonesome and tries to call for help."

Liddell led the way back to the companionway amidships. They descended noiselessly into the interior of the boat. From some place near by came the unmistakable sounds of a transmitter in action. Liddell motioned for Herlehy to follow, walked slowly to the room housing the transmitter.

At the closed door to the room, Liddell paused, put his ear to the panel, nodded. "They're sending." He tried the knob. It turned easily in his hand. He pushed the door open a crack.

Ben Cerla sat at the transmitting apparatus, earphones on his head. Leaning over him was the elusive Goldy. Cerla was sending a code signal, stopped every few seconds, wiped his brow with the back of his hand.

"Looks like they haven't gotten through to their contact yet," Liddell whispered. "Let's take them."

He pushed the door wider, slid through, Herlehy followed.

At the transmitter, Cerla was sending his code signal frantically. Liddell started toward the apparatus, gun in hand, when he felt the snout of a revolver poked in his back. He whirled, gun at ready, to stare down the barrel of a .45. Behind him, Herlehy stood also looking into the barrel of a .45.

The two hard-eyed men behind the .45's relieved Liddell and the inspector of their guns.

At the sending apparatus, Cerla stiffened, exclaimed aloud. He bent over it, answered the chatter of the receiver with a flood of code. The receiver chattered back, Cerla relaxed.

"I've gotten through." He looked up at Goldy. From the corner of his eye, he caught sight of Liddell. The look of surprise was frozen on his face when Goldy lifted her arm; there was a flash of metal, and Cerla toppled from the chair as she brought the barrel of her gun down on his head.

The man behind Liddell hurried forward, slid into Cerla's seat, adjusted the earphones, took over the sending apparatus. Goldy covered Liddell with an ugly, short barreled .38.

Liddell estimated his chances for getting through long enough to smash the sending set, was deterred by the steadiness of Goldy's arm. After a moment the receiving unit started to chatter wildly. The man at the shortwave set answered in code, repeated much of what he had sent previously. The receiver chattered its confirmation, then stopped abruptly.

The man at the sending set got up from his chair, slipped off Cerla's earphones. Then, pulling out his gun he set about smashing the instruments.

"Get the whole message through?" Goldy asked.

The man at the set nodded. "The whole thing. They even had me repeat to make sure they got the formula right." He picked up a piece of paper he had made a series of notes on. "Got a lot of instructions to be passed along to key agents throughout the country, too. Names, places, assignments."

For a moment, Goldy turned her attention from Liddell. He started a jump for her, was knocked off balance by the man guarding Herlehy.

"Get him, Herlehy," Liddell shouted. "You heard them. They were sending secret information and formulas abroad. They're spies."

Goldy laughed nasally. "That's right, inspector. We were sending out the formula for a new bomb." She threw back her head, laughed loudly. "I hope when they put it together they're in the middle of the desert. We forgot to tell them that there's no way to keep it from going off once it's assembled."

Liddell stared at the woman, transferred his gaze to the man at the sending set. "What is this?"

"A trap, Liddell," the man told him. "A trap for a gang of espionage and terrorist agents working in this country." He fished into an inside pocket, brought out a leather folder, flipped it open, revealed a Treasury Department badge. "I'm attached to the counterespionage division of the Secret Service. "So's he," he nodded to the man standing beside Herlehy.

"But her—*she's a spy!* She was behind the whole thing," Liddell pointed to Goldy.

"Not the way you think, Liddell," the T-man told him. "She's been working with us ever since this thing started. She was the one that sicked Treasury on Brin and Cerla for shaking down the Chinese."

Liddell growled under his breath. "Then why didn't you move in on them and knock them off?"

"Impatient, ain't he?" Goldy grinned.

The T-man shrugged. "We found they were engaged in a lot worse than shaking down Chinese. Espionage."

Liddell smote his head with the flat of his hand, groaned.

"Then she was working *with* Hong. She didn't kill him?"

Goldy shook her head. "Kill that little guy? I could tear the rat that did it apart with my hands," she growled nasally. "For a little old guy he had more cold nerve than anybody ten times his size I ever seen."

The T-man nodded. "He got the gang's code. That was what he left for us in the package in your office. But we couldn't use it until now."

"Why not?" Liddell growled.

Goldy stirred the unconscious body of Cerla. "We had the code, but we didn't have the password. We needed one of these rats to set up contact with the scum he's been working for."

Liddell groaned. "You guys gotta work along with me and keep this under your hats. If this ever gets out, I—"

From the outside corridor came a hooting laugh. "This I wouldn't have missed for the world! Johnny Liddell arrests the counterespionage service for espionage. What a story! And the *Advance* has got it exclusive!" It was Muggsy Kiely's voice.

Liddell squirmed uncomfortably on the hard wooden chair in the cubbyhole allotted to Treasury Agent Byers in the federal building. He made a determined effort not to look in the direction of Muggsy Kiely's smirking face. His only consolation was the knowledge that farther uptown, in his cubbyhole at headquarters, Inspector Herlehy was squirming just as uncomfortably.

Byers leaned back, verified much of what the T-man had told Liddell of Goldy's part in smashing the ring.

"They thought she'd be useful to them because of her contacts with the Chinese," he concluded. "But instead she immediately contacted us. We assigned Hong to work with her."

"That was why she had Hong's picture, Johnny. So she'd know him when he made contact," Muggsy offered brightly.

Liddell nodded testily. "Even I've been able to figure that one. That's also why we found it left in the apartment. Goldy didn't pack her own things. The mob stuck her under cover, sent one of their own boys to get her stuff."

Byers nodded. "That's exactly what did happen, Liddell." He picked a pipe from his rack, started filling it with tobacco. "You know the reason she was forced to go under cover was the fact that you'd recognized her at Brin's party, don't you?"

Liddell nodded.

"That's why we didn't want you to get into the case in the first place," Byers continued. "We had it pretty well sewed up and we didn't want Goldy getting the same medicine from the gang that poor old Hong got." He put the pipe between his teeth, scratched a match, applied it. "We couldn't, of course, jeopardize her life by telling you she was working with us. And we were scared stiff you'd kick the whole thing over by grabbing her and arresting her. Or worse." He filled the air over his head with a thick cloud of dark-blue smoke. "Your having a client gave us a bad moment. We couldn't force you to pull out of the case without explaining to him, so we decided to let you go along." He grinned bleakly. "That decision was rather fatal to several people—Lunfaro, Brin, and his bodyguard."

"No great loss," Liddell growled. He got up from his chair. "I guess I'd better run along."

Byers rose, extended his hand. "No hard feelings, Liddell. You understand we couldn't tip you off."

"Might've saved me from making a jerk of myself." Liddell grinned rucfully. "I thought I had it figured out all so neat." He shrugged. "Just goes to show you. Coming, Muggsy?"

The reporter nodded perkily. "Think you can get away without me? I want a firsthand story on how it feels to expose the FBI as a spy ring." Liddell shuddered; Muggsy giggled. "Sorry, Liddell, but you did stick your neck out." She shook hands with Byers.

"Okay, okay. So I stuck my neck out. Take a tip from a guy who knows, Muggs. Don't ever do it." He jammed his hat on his head, stamped out.

"Where you going, Liddell?" Muggsy called after him. "Wait for me."

"I can't," Liddell called back over his shoulder. "I just remembered I have to report to my client. And I get nervous in front of witnesses!"

CHAPTER SEVENTEEN

JOHNNY LIDDELL PACED the area surrounding the table in Jimmy Kaiming's office. He broke off his pacing to glower at his client, who sat relaxed, cigarette holder tilted from the corner of his mouth.

"I blew the whole thing. Just like an amateur," he growled. "I got off on a wrong scent and ran around in circles like a punched-up bird dog."

Kaiming made a gesture of deprecation. "You could not have known this woman was an undercover agent. No one could have known."

Liddell stamped over to the chair opposite Kaiming's, dropped into it. "It all fitted together so neatly. It had to be someone who knew the Chinese intimately enough to know where their relatives were located in China. Cerla didn't have that kind of information. Neither did Brin. It looked like it had to be her."

Kaiming nodded, clapped his hands. Fah Soo appeared, smiling and bowing. "Mr. Liddell would like some refreshments, I think," Kaiming told the girl.

Fah Soo bowed, left the room.

"I almost had the truth when Brin was killed. For that matter, I almost had it before Lunfaro was killed," Liddell growled. "It was a case of almosts."

Kaiming shrugged. "Bad luck, no doubt."

The girl returned, placed a bottle and some glasses on the table, stood aside.

"After all, you did get what you went after, Hong's killer," Kaiming reminded him.

"Which one was it?" Liddell growled.

"Does it make much difference?" Kaiming shrugged. "Whoever it was, he is either dead or in jail."

"That would mean that either Cerla or Brin was behind this whole operation." Liddell grunted. "Neither of them was."

Kaiming raised his eyebrows. "Why do you say that?"

"They didn't fill the specifications. Make the contacts to steal or buy military secrets, yes. Make the contacts for setting up the ransom ring, maybe. Have the necessary background and entree into Chinatown, no."

Fah Soo bent over the table, spilled some of the liquid from the bottle into Liddell's glass.

Kaiming removed the cigarette holder from between his teeth, removed the butt, crushed it out. "Who then?"

Liddell took the glass from the outstretched hand of the girl, shrugged. "Let's take another look at this character. It's somebody who knew the old-country connections of the local Chinese. Somebody who knew I was on the case, was able to put a tail on me, thus know that I was close to Lunfaro and Brin," he tabulated. "It was somebody who knew that I had seen Goldy in the house where Hong was killed, who would thus know I had recognized her at Brin's party. It was somebody who could get Cerla and Goldy hidden out in the heart of Chinatown."

Kaiming pursed his lips thoughtfully. "A very powerful person."

Liddell nodded. "A tong leader usually is."

Kaiming looked tired. "You suspect me? How ridiculous."

"Not very. It was ridiculous that I didn't suspect you before now. Your tong was licked in the last tong war. You told me that yourself. That means you lost the concession to run the Fan-Tan. You lost opium rights and the best locations for restaurants and other rackets. In other words, your tong was practically broke." He looked around. "This place cost a fortune and some of those gimcracks in the other room two fortunes. So, obviously, you've hit on some source of revenue. It isn't legit or the other tong would have taken it over."

"Very ingenious."

Liddell nodded. "More ingenious than for you to arrange to have someone waiting for me in that passage behind the Fan Tan game. No one but you could have known I was on my way over there. Why didn't you finish me there?"

Kaiming looked up at the fragile Chinese girl. "Why indeed? Perhaps the lovely Fah Soo would care to explain."

The Chinese girl bared her teeth in a cruel smile. "I did not know the yellow-haired one was not one of us. She promised it would be done. I trusted her."

Liddell nodded. "Then it was you who sapped me. It had to be, of course."

The girl nodded. "My great regret is that this arm lacked the strength to finish the job." She indicated the glass in Liddell's hand. "Drink. It will be easier that way."

Liddell sniffed the glass, wrinkled his nose. "Poisoned, eh?"

Kaiming didn't look up, fitted a cigarette to his holder.

"Would you perhaps prefer to go as the old one went, the one you call Hong?" Fah Soo smiled her cruel smile. "It was not easy, it was not fast. He was stubborn, the old one. He died without telling where he had left the package."

"How did you find out I had it?"

"You told us, Liddell," Kaiming put in. "You came here right after Hong's death, told us you had been hired by him. It was obvious that he had left the package with you."

Liddell nodded. "Very obvious. But why send a white killer after me? Why not one of your own?"

Fah Soo grinned. "The American Chinese are soft. They can not do their own killing. The day of the hatchet man is past. Their own gunmen do not shoot straight. We are forced to hire the white killers to have the job done right."

"But you put in a couple of personal touches of your own, Fah Soo. Hong. Brin, too, I guess, eh?"

The girl shrugged. "He was a fool. He threatened to talk to save his own hide."

Kaiming sighed softly. "She is right, Liddell. Drink. It will be faster, more merciful." He glanced up at the girl. "Where she comes from they do not know the meaning of mercy."

The girl glanced at him with distrust. "It is well my superiors sent me here—to keep an eye on weaklings such as you. You are willing to take our gold, but you cringe at the work you must do to earn it."

"You're right, Liddell. My tong has lost its power. I thought to ally myself with the new order in China, to capitalize on the support and money they could give me. I saw myself once again all-powerful in Chinatown." He sighed. "They never meant it to be. They only meant to use me until they had taken over here, then I was through."

"You will be dealt with properly by my superiors." Fah Soo curled her lip at the tong leader.

Liddell put the glass down on the table. "Take it easy, Mata Hari. The third act's almost over. The cavalry should come charging to the rescue any minute."

The girl's hand receded into the voluminous sleeve, reappeared with a small but efficient-looking automatic. "You prefer it my way? So be it. It will be pleasant to hear you scream for mercy."

Liddell grinned. "Too bad you can't have it recorded for propaganda purposes, eh, baby?" He glanced toward the transparent door. "Keep your eye on the door for a moment."

The girl sneered. "You bluff. You Americans are expert at bluffing."

"That's a pretty substantial bluff." Liddell indicated the glass door. Outside a group of men had appeared. They were armed with axes and crowbars. The glass of the door started to split and crack under the fury of their blows.

"It's no bluff, Fah Soo," Kaiming yelled. "We can still make it out the back way."

Liddell shook his head. "I remembered how it worked, so I passed the word along to the feds, Kaiming. You're boxed. But good."

The color had drained from the normally pale face of the woman, leaving her eyes and mouth as dark shadows in the pallor. Her lips had drawn away from her teeth in an animal-like snarl. "So be it. But you're coming with us, Liddell." She raised the gun, aimed.

Almost simultaneously, Liddell threw himself forward. He heard the roar of the gun, felt the sear of the bullet as it grazed his shoulder. His bulk hit the girl, sent her sprawling.

Outside, the sledgehammers were smashing the thick door from its hinges. Liddell had his hands full with the squirming, scratching fury he was trying to tame. Suddenly, he brought his fist up, felt it connect with her jaw with paralyzing force. Fah Soo's body went limp.

Liddell got up, brushed himself off, looked down at the unconscious form. "I apologize, baby. I'm no gentleman." He felt for the slight wound in his shoulder. "No gentleman would think of hitting a lady without first taking off his hat."

There was a gasping for breath behind him. Kaiming sat in the chair, a film forming over his eyes, a glass in his hand. A slight dribble of saliva showed at the corners of his mouth, ran down his chin. The glass slipped through his fingers, smashed on the floor.

"Your drink, Liddell," he gasped. "I hope you don't mind—my drinking your drink."

His jaw sagged, his arm fell to his side. His eyes were still open, but the film over them had become opaque.

The glass of the door finally gave way, and a wave of plainclothes men poured in. Byers, the Treasury Department man, walked over to Liddell. "You okay. Johnny?"

Liddell nodded, indicated the scratch on his shoulder. "She was right. They do have to hire white gunmen who can shoot straight."

Byers took a look at the wound, seemed satisfied. "You were right, too. We've got enough on Kaiming to tag him for sure as the head of the espionage ring."

Liddell pointed to Kaiming. "You're too late. He's dead." He indicated the unconscious girl. "Here was his real boss, though, NKVD Chinese-style. Sent here to supervise his activities. He started out shaking the local Chinese for ransom. She was the one that added the espionage to the agenda."

Byers nodded. "You know this all the time?"

"Hell, no," Liddell groaned. "It added up when I sat down and checked back. Where I made my mistake was adding apples and oranges. All you get that way is fruit salad. When I got around to adding just apples, everything cleared up." He started to pour a drink from the bottle, pulled his hand away as though it was hot. "Everything that I had that pointed to Goldy pointed to Kaiming as well. So, if it wasn't Goldy it had to be Kaiming." He shrugged. "Just like that."

"You did a nice job, Liddell," Byers told him. "We can clean up around here. No need of you hanging around if you've got anything else to do."

"Meaning?"

Byers grinned. "I tipped off that blond newshawk gal of yours that you might be having a story for her. I think she's probably waiting for you at her place."

Jim Kiely was sitting on the terrace with Muggsy when Johnny Liddell walked in. He grinned at Liddell. "Hear you've been giving the federal boys a bad time, Johnny." He made room on the settee for Liddell, didn't seem perturbed when the detective elected to perch on the arm of Muggsy's chair. "What's this I hear about you almost snafuing their smashing of the spy ring?"

Liddell grinned. "Muggs been talking? Why don't you run that story in that rag of yours so I can sue you for libel?"

"And lose me my job?" Muggsy pouted.

"Why not?" Liddell nodded. "No wife of mine is going to work."

Muggsy shook her head positively. "And no husband of mine is going to be a second-string shooting-gallery. If I give up my racket, you've got to give up yours." She dropped her eyes. "You're probably washed up now, anyhow."

"Maybe," Liddell conceded. "Although Byers didn't seem to think so when I gave him Kaiming with practically a confession. In fact, he sounded downright grateful."

Muggsy looked up, her jaw hanging. "Kaiming? What's he got to do with it?"

Liddell reached over, snagged her half-full glass, drained it. "What's Kaiming got to do with it, she asks! He had everything to do with it. He was head of the ring." He snapped his fingers. "Say, I did forget to mention that to you, didn't I?"

Jim Kiely jumped up from the couch so fast he spilled his drink all over the rug. He grabbed a phone, started dialing. "You got the whole story, Johnny?"

"Sure I got the whole story." Liddell grinned. "I had it all along. Only trouble was I was looking at it from the wrong angle. Once I got my sights adjusted, everything fell in line."

Jim Kiely was barking orders into the telephone. He put the receiver down, grabbed Liddell by the arm. "Never mind telling us about it. Start talking into that," he pointed to the phone.

Liddell grinned, shrugged. "Okay." He picked up the phone. "Rewrite?" The receiver barked assent. "Just slug this with Ronny Kiely's by-line." He leaned back, got comfortable, started dictating. After about fifteen minutes, he hung the receiver up, rubbed his ear.

"What a yarn!" Jim Kiely exulted. "I should have known you'd come out on top. Like I told Muggs—"

Muggsy came in from the kitchen with half a carcass of chicken. Solemnly, she sat cross-legged on the settee, gnawed at the bones.

"I'm sorry we have no crow in the house, Johnny. This'll have to do."

THE END

If you've enjoyed this book, you will not want to miss these terrific titles...

ARMCHAIR MYSTERY & SCIENCE FICTION CLASSICS
$12.95 each

C-40 **MODEL FOR MURDER**
by Stephen Marlowe

C-41 **PRELUDE TO MURDER**
by Sterling Noel

C-42 **DEAD WEIGHT**
by Frank Kane

C-43 **A DAME CALLED MURDER**
by Milton Ozaki

C-44 **THE GREATEST ADVENTURE**
by John Taine

C-45 **THE EXILE OF TIME**
by Ray Cummings

C-46 **STORM OVER WARLOCK**
by Andre Norton

C-47 **MAN OF MANY MINDS**
by E. Everett Evans

C-48 **THE GODS OF MARS**
by Edgar Rice Burroughs

C-49 **BRIGANDS OF THE MOON**
by Ray Cummings

C-50 **SPACE HOUNDS OF IPC**
by E. E. "Doc" Smith

C-51 **THE LANI PEOPLE**
by J. F. Bone

C-52 **THE MOON POOL**
by A. Merritt

C-53 **IN THE DAYS OF THE COMET**
by H. G. Wells

C-54 **TRIPLANETARY**
E. E. Doc Smith

If you've enjoyed this book, you will not want to miss these terrific titles...

ARMCHAIR SCI-FI & HORROR DOUBLE NOVELS, $12.95 each

D-91 **THE TIME TRAP** by Henry Kuttner
THE LUNAR LICHEN by Hal Clement

D-92 **SARGASSO OF LOST STARSHIPS** by Poul Anderson
THE ICE QUEEN by Don Wilcox

D-93 **THE PRINCE OF SPACE** by Jack Williamson
POWER by Harl Vincent

D-94 **PLANET OF NO RETURN** by Howard Browne
THE ANNIHILATOR COMES by Ed Earl Repp

D-95 **THE SINISTER INVASION** by Edmond Hamilton
OPERATION TERROR by Murray Leinster

D-96 **TRANSIENT** by Ward Moore
THE WORLD-MOVER by George O. Smith

D-97 **FORTY DAYS HAS SEPTEMBER** by Milton Lesser
THE DEVIL'S PLANET by David Wright O'Brien

D-98 **THE CYBERENE** by Rog Phillips
BADGE OF INFAMY by Lester del Rey

D-99 **THE JUSTICE OF MARTIN BRAND** by Raymond A. Palmer
BRING BACK MY BRAIN by Dwight V. Swain

D-100 **WIDE-OPEN PLANET** by L. Sprague de Camp
AND THEN THE TOWN TOOK OFF by Richard Wilson

ARMCHAIR SCIENCE FICTION CLASSICS, $12.95 each

C-31 **THE GOLDEN GUARDSMEN**
by S. J. Byrne

C-32 **ONE AGAINST THE MOON**
by Donald A. Wollheim

C-33 **HIDDEN CITY**
by Chester S. Geier

ARMCHAIR SCI-FI & HORROR GEMS SERIES, $12.95 each

G-9 **SCIENCE FICTION GEMS, Vol. Five**
Clifford D. Simak and others

G-10 **HORROR GEMS, Vol. Five**
E. Hoffman Price and others

If you've enjoyed this book, you will not want to miss these terrific titles…

ARMCHAIR SCI-FI & HORROR DOUBLE NOVELS, $12.95 each

D-101   **THE CONQUEST OF THE PLANETS** by John W. Campbell
        THE MAN WHO ANNEXED THE MOON by Bob Olsen

D-102   **WEAPON FROM THE STARS** by Rog Phillips
        THE EARTH WAR by Mack Reynolds

D-103   **THE ALIEN INTELLIGENCE** by Jack Williamson
        INTO THE FOURTH DIMENSION by Ray Cummings

D-104   **THE CRYSTAL PLANETOIDS** by Stanton A. Coblentz
        SURVIVORS FROM 9,000 B. C. by Robert Moore Williams

D-105   **THE TIME PROJECTOR** by David H. Keller, M.D. and David Lasser
        STRANGE COMPULSION by Philip Jose Farmer

D-106   **WHOM THE GODS WOULD SLAY** by Paul W. Fairman
        MEN IN THE WALLS by William Tenn

D-107   **LOCKED WORLDS** by Edmond Hamilton
        THE LAND THAT TIME FORGOT by Edgar Rice Burroughs

D-108   **STAY OUT OF SPACE** by Dwight V. Swain
        REBELS OF THE RED PLANET by Charles L. Fontenay

D-109   **THE METAMORPHS** by S. J. Byrne
        MICROCOSMIC BUCCANEERS by Harl Vincent

D-110   **YOU CAN'T ESCAPE FROM MARS** by E. K. Jarvis
        THE MAN WITH FIVE LIVES by David V. Reed

ARMCHAIR SCIENCE FICTION CLASSICS, $12.95 each

C-34   **30 DAY WONDER**
       by Richard Wilson

C-35   **G.O.G. 666**
       by John Taine

C-36   **RALPH 124C 41+**
       by Hugo Gernsback

ARMCHAIR SCI-FI & HORROR GEMS SERIES, $12.95 each

G-11   **SCIENCE FICTION GEMS, Vol. Six**
       Edmond Hamilton and others

G-12   **HORROR GEMS, Vol. Six**
       H. P. Lovecraft and others

If you've enjoyed this book, you will not want to miss these terrific titles…

ARMCHAIR SCI-FI & HORROR DOUBLE NOVELS, $12.95 each

D-111 **THE MOON ERA** by Jack Williamson
        REVENGE OF THE ROBOTS by Howard Browne

D-112 **SON OF THE BLACK CHALICE** by Milton Lesser
        SENTRY OF THE SKY by Evelyn E. Smith

D-113 **OUTPOST ON THE MOON** by Joslyn Maxwell
        POTENTIAL ZERO by S. J. Byrne

D-114 **OUTPOST INFINITY** by Raymond F. Jones
        THE WHITE INVADERS by Ray Cummings

D-115 **TIME TRAP** by Rog Phillips
        THE COSMIC DESTROYER by Alexander Blade

D-116 **THE OTHER SIDE OF THE MOON** by Edmond Hamilton
        SECRET INVASION by Walter Kubilius

D-117 **DANGER MOON** by Frederik Pohl
        THE HIDDEN UNIVERSE by Ralph Milne Farley

D-118 **THE WAILING ASTEROID** by Murray Leinster
        THE WORLD THAT COULDN'T BE by Clifford D. Simak

D-119 **THE WHISPERING GORILLA** by Don Wilcox
        RETURN OF THE WHISPERING GORILLA by David V. Reed

D-120 **SPECIAL EFFECT** by J. F. Bone
        WARLORD OF KOR by Terry Carr

ARMCHAIR SCIENCE FICTION CLASSICS, $12.95 each

C-37   **THE GREEN MAN RETURNS**
        by Harold M. Sherman

C-38   **THE SHAVER MYSTERY, Book Five**
        by Richard S, Shaver

C-39   **MARS CHILD**
        by Cyril Judd

ARMCHAIR MASTERS OF SCIENCE FICTION SERIES, $16.95 each

MS-9   **MASTERS OF SCIENCE FICTION AND FANTASY, Vol. Nine**
        Poul Anderson, "The Star Beast" and other tales

MS-10 **MASTERS OF SCIENCE FICTION, Vol. Ten**
        Robert Moore Williams, "Time Tolls for Toro" and other tales